Three Children

Lori Toppel

SUMMIT BOOKS

New York   London   Toronto   Sydney   Tokyo   Singapore

SUMMIT BOOKS
Simon & Schuster Building
Rockefeller Center
1230 Avenue of the Americas
New York, New York, 10020

DESIGNED BY MARC STRANG
Manufactured in the United States of America

1   3   5   7   9   10   8   6   4   2

Library of Congress Cataloging in Publication Data

Toppel, Lori.
Three children / Lori Toppel.
p.   cm.
I. Title.
PS3570.0657T48   1992
813'.54—dc20   91-33817
                                                    CIP

ISBN 0-671-73959-X

97,676
capman
$ 20.00

Acknowledgments

*My deepest affection and gratitude to
Ben Sonnenberg, teacher and friend.*

*And many thanks to
Georges Borchardt and Ileene Smith.*
                                    L. T.

For my father, my mother, and my sister

Contents

PART THREE

Part One

Rebecca's Theory

I trust water. I know my limitations in water. And I don't press beyond them. My name is Clarissa; I'm twenty-five. Lately, I swim a lot. Swimming toughens the vital organs: lungs and heart. A swallow of air measures every stroke. When I'm underwater, I can't see or hear clearly and can't smell anything. I'm humble. I'm forgiving with others and myself. Maybe I'd have been better off living somewhere like Cuzco, in Peru, when it was the capital of the Inca. Water streamed down from the Andes and flowed in ditches throughout the city. When hot, I'd have knelt under a fountain. A vicuña would have sipped at a trough near my feet. More often, I think of another place, Atlantis. That is my favorite myth. The island was rich and no doubt lush. But I imagine its splendor after an earthquake sank it.

My grandmother was afraid of the water. She never swam. Her name was Rebecca Lyon, always known to us as Nanny. She was my father's mother and the only grandparent I ever met. I know little about my mother's past. She tells me that she lost both her parents during the Second World War. She is British and her name is Julia.

My father, David, was brought up in Hidden Gorge, a small town in upstate New York. His father ran a nine-hundred-square-foot grocery store called The Lyon Den Mart. The family lived on top. In 1952, my grandfather died of a heart attack. A few months later, Nanny gave my father and his sister enough money to build a supermarket in Puerto Rico. At the time, the island had only small grocery stores, or *colmados*. Nadia, my father's sister, moved to Puerto Rico shortly after my father did. Today they have several stores on the island and throughout the Caribbean: in Saint John, Saint Thomas, Saint Croix, Tortola and Venezuela. They named the supermarkets Isla.

As our father puts it, my brother, my sister and I are "pampered." We've been given some money. Sometimes we justify our good fortune by feeling guilty. The guilt lets us pretend we're noble. Our father is sometimes noble. A friend of his once said, "Your dad is one of the few honest people left on earth." He appears to find a goodness in almost every man he meets. But he's not always sociable. He likes small islands where there are few people. Maybe that's his way of pretending he has only himself to answer to.

I look like my father. I'm tall and my skin is more olive than white. Like him, I have a high forehead and a dimple on my left cheek when I smile. He tells me I also have his poise. I keep my chin high; I'm never clumsy.

I grew up in a small suburb of Puerto Rico called Santa María. Our house had white gates, or *rejas*, Spanish ceramic roof tiles, white plaster walls and a cupola with a horse weather vane. I was born in 1955 and stayed an only child for four years.

Nanny kept me company. She visited me every week. She drove in from Santurce, where she lived with her housekeeper. Nanny would bounce me high on her knee. She taught me gin rummy. She'd slap down cards. She'd say, I win, over and over. The day I won, she accused me of cheating.

In September 1959, Cora was born. She doesn't look like me. She has blue eyes, like our father's. Otherwise, she looks like our mother. She has her round face and fair skin. She is small-boned.

Michael came a year after Cora. As a baby he had straight blond hair. When it turned dark brown, I remember thinking he looked a lot like my brother. He grew to be six feet. But he doesn't seem big. His legs, his neck, his fingers are all slender and almost graceful.

Nanny's attentions turned to Cora and Michael. So I started to lie. I told my sister and brother stories of what I'd done before they were born. I told them I rode an albino horse in the rain; I cantered for hours. I told them I took a helicopter to a volcano top in Sicily; the volcano had just erupted. I told them stories of what I'd just read as if they were true. I read a lot. My mother had given me reading lessons every morning since I was three. I taught Cora and Michael how to read. I wanted them to look up to me. Nanny taught them how to play cards.

When I was six, my father found me a piano teacher. He was a short man with a red mustache. He used to carry a stack of old music sheets under his arm. He made me copy the music by hand. He used to tell me, "You're the kind of student who can't become too polished. You'll lose your gut feeling for the music." We had a Pianola. When I wasn't playing, my mother pedaled it. We'd all sing to "Caravan," "Stella by Starlight," "Making Whoopee." But the Pianola was eight keys short. My teacher never complained. He said I practiced a lot and that was all he could ask for.

I liked the certainty of notes. They were less ambiguous than words. When I made a mistake, I knew it right away. The fewer mistakes I made, the more Nanny cooed. She began taking me on her lap again. I played with her under me. She made Cora and Michael stand next to me and listen. Nanny said I was a natural musician; I was meant to be a famous pianist. But I never thought of myself as gifted.

*   *   *

The year Nanny turned ninety, she came to visit for a few days.
I was eight. My mother took us to the supermarket. Nanny
frightened me: she began ranting about tomatoes and lettuces
tumbling out of the bins. She said there were rats in the aisles
poking their snouts at her toes. My mother had no desire to
listen to her. So she drove her to my father's office. She told him
to take her home. Then my mother picked up our housekeeper,
Rosa, and drove us all to the Japanese gardens, almost an hour
away.

The gardens were in a hotel off a San Juan beach. The hotel
was always busy with businessmen and tourists. Cubans and Eu-
ropeans gambled in the casino. They sauntered on the garden
paths. Cora and I watched them as if to learn from their motions.
My mother called certain women the "gentry." They were pearl-
skinned and had black hair. Descendants, my mother said, of the
conquistadores. One or two such women lived in Santa María. My
mother knew them but thought they were too proud.

We entered the garden from the north on a path of stones laid
in the grass. The path snaked up a hill. On top of the hill there
was a pond with lily pads. A wooden gazebo with a bridge had
been built in the middle of the pond. The gazebo was our sanc-
tuary. We had picnics there. Then we threw bread crumbs to the
garden birds. Pelicans balanced on one leg; peacocks dragged
their tails in the grass; ducks stepped in and out of the pond. The
pond streamed over the south side of the hill and turned into a
waterfall. Cora, Michael and I used to roll down a dry part of the
hill. At the bottom there was an abandoned art gallery, rotting
under a mango tree. We used to play around the gallery.

Mom said to Rosa, "What a relief to escape that Rebecca." We
were sitting in the gazebo. It was almost five, and we'd been at
the gardens since noon.

Rosa was from Peru. She'd been with us since I was three.
She'd learned English for Mom. But Michael, Cora and I liked to
talk to her in Spanish. Her clothes smelled of garlic. Her skin

smelled like pine. She had a flat nose and paper-thin ears. The whites of her eyes had yellow shades in them. She was showing Michael how to whistle with a blade of grass. I was bent over the pond, catching guppies in a paper cup. Cora sat Indian-style next to me. She wore a yellow dress she'd already soiled.

"Rosa, that woman keeps him up all night sometimes," Mom said and lit a cigarette. "She was a wild one. She had her men. Plenty, too. She loves to tell me all about them."

Rosa said, "Doña Rebecca is a good woman. She doesn't know what she says."

"She knows exactly what she's saying. She told me I should stop trying to have children. Imagine! Now she's begun this raving. Don't underestimate her power, Rosa. That was my mistake. She's a mighty one."

Mom caught me listening and blew me a kiss. She wore her hair short and behind her ears. Her hair is blond-red and her eyes are green; the left one slopes down a little. When angry, she closes both eyes halfway.

She took off her hat and fanned herself with it. Even in the shade Mom felt the heat. She left to call Dad. When she returned, she said, "I told your father we'd be late. I packed sweaters in case it gets chilly."

Cora leaned forward to watch the guppies writhing in the cup. She said, "Do we have to wait until dark? After dark, God comes out."

I giggled. I didn't believe in God. My father made me go to Hebrew school. I skipped lessons. I never liked the quiet of synagogues, the small talk after the services. Passover or Yom Kippur was a chore to me. My mother is Catholic. She has, to all appearances, converted. Yet when frightened or nervous, she crosses herself.

"I have some juice and cookies," Mom said.

"Let's leave before it's dark," Cora said.

"Have a go at more of those tadpoles."

"Doña Julia," Rosa said, "Michael hasn't had his nap."

And Mom said, "He'll live."

Cora and I headed for the waterfall at the bottom of the hill. We splattered our ankles in the mango pulp and mud. We looked through a cracked window of the art gallery. I said, "Look at the shadows on the pedestals. Let's go in." We'd never been inside.

Cora didn't want to. I said I'd go in myself and she changed her mind. We crawled through a window. The glass was missing. There were two rooms. The back one had a dirty desk in it. I sat behind the desk and pretended to play Mozart.

"Look at me," I heard Cora shout.

In the other room, she'd climbed onto a pedestal. She was holding her hands up. She looked like a skinny cherub. I climbed onto a larger pedestal and thought there was no way a living thing could look like art.

Mom came to the window and watched us.

When we got home, she said, "You looked so quiet. Just like statues. I couldn't disturb you."

Standing on the pedestal made me feel composed. My mother would tell me she always sees me that way. She believes people like to assess our graces. I believe we ask people to judge us. Sometimes we even insist.

Michael fell asleep during dinner. Rosa carried him to his room. His room was blue, with white floors and a white ceiling. His bed was near the window. He could look out to the top of palm trees and the sky. I liked where his room was: above Mom and Dad's and between Cora's and mine. My room faced the backyard, the pool and the forest that belonged to the church. We had a flamboyan tree. When the tree was flowering, I didn't mind my view.

Nanny ate slowly. She toyed with the lacy collar of her yellow robe. Her face was long and smooth. Her eyes seemed to have clouds in them. She said to Dad, "Did you make sure the bulbs were changed in the store?"

He said, "The stores are very bright."

Nanny chewed for a long time and then said, "Your grandfather, Clarissa, he was smart." She winked at me. "He never let a light burn out. Smart . . . How were the gardens?" she said to Mom.

"Empty and quite lovely, but they should do something about that art gallery. It's beginning to smell."

"Worry if it doesn't smell," Nanny said. "One of the most beautiful things I've ever seen stank like hell. It was a whale in the straits off Vancouver Island."

We'd already heard about the boat trip Nanny and my grandfather had taken. A whale had breached a mile away. Later, on Vancouver Island, she'd bought my parents a white and gray marble whale. Mom stored the whale in the closet. She took it out when Nanny visited.

Nanny pointed to the whale on the coffee table. She said, "One of the most beautiful sights, and it stank like hell."

I wondered how a whale could smell if the sea rinsed it over and over again.

Mom trimmed her steak. But then she ate the fat instead of the meat. She held her napkin to her mouth while she coughed.

"Then there are baby elephants," Nanny said. "Their mothers smell them all around when they're asleep. To make sure they're alive. So, my Julia, worry if it doesn't smell."

"They shouldn't keep babies in a zoo," Cora said.

Everyone was asleep, but I writhed in bed, feeling sunburned. I went into the living room. Mosquitoes were swarming around the lamp. The terrace door was open. I went to close it. It was cool outside and I walked toward the pool. The pool lights were on. I spotted a shadow in the deep end. Nanny floated face down in a yellow gown. Her head and upper body had sunk deeper than her legs. I jumped in, but I couldn't swim to her. I became scared. I went back to the house. I woke up Mom and Dad. They both put on their robes and ran barefoot to the pool.

Dad started to pull Nanny out. Mom switched on all the lights in the poolhouse. "David, just leave her," she said. "The ambulance will do it. Just leave her."

I thought I saw something gray at the bottom of the pool.

Mom said to me, "Please get back in the house."

I tried to figure out how Nanny had ended up in the pool. Had anyone wanted to hurt her? Had she been sleepwalking? Or had she drowned herself?

Cora and Michael came skipping across the yard. They were holding hands. Michael in his red pajamas, Cora in a white nightgown. Cora gathered a fistful of nightgown and stood behind Mom. She said, "Oh, that looks like Nanny." Then she began giggling. Mom lifted her. Cora kept saying, "God got her."

There were ten services for Nanny. I wanted to go to all ten. That was impossible, Dad explained: they'd all take place at noon.

"Why are there so many?" I said.

"Puerto Rico didn't have any modern supermarkets before Isla came," he said. "The people here are grateful for the food we brought. And for the jobs. So all the people, all over the island, want to thank Nanny." I liked how Nanny had made it possible for people to get what they needed.

Dad told me some of the towns didn't have a temple. The service in Yauco would be in a community service building. The service in Toa Baja would be in a church. We were driving to the temple in Santurce, where the first Isla store had been built. I sat between Mom and Dad.

"Listen to me," Dad said, taking one hand off the steering wheel to hold my shoulder. "Nanny didn't feel right the night she died. She didn't mean to do what she did. There's a difference between losing hope and being confused."

"Haven't we talked about this enough?" Mom said. She sounded scared. She was powdering her nose. Then she powdered mine, too.

A sign outside the temple read: SERVICES FOR REBECCA LYON. We hurried in and found seats. I recognized a reverend who'd been at the last store opening with the rabbi. The rabbi was talking to Aunt Nadia and Dad. The reverend handed a thin stack of papers to Mom, who was the first person in our row. Mom told me to take one of the papers and pass the rest down the bench. Printed on the paper was a list of all the towns honoring Nanny at noon. Río Piedras, Bayamón, Puerto Nuevo, Toa Baja, Ponce, Fajardo, Caguas, Yauco (where was Yauco?) Humacao and Guaynabo. I whispered the names quickly to my-self, over and over. I wanted to give Nanny a name that sounded as important as these towns. Grandmother Rebecca. Grand-mother Rebecca rose through the floor of the supermarket. She checked for rats. She picked up lettuce. I listened to the rabbi: . . . *and she died by an accident not even God could prevent.* . . .

The services were short. Some people crossed themselves be-fore leaving. I asked a few people if they'd met my grandmother. I counted how many had. I shook everyone's hand. Then I snuck outside and sat on the curb. I was sorry I hadn't been able to save Grandmother Rebecca. I was sorry Mom had talked behind Grandmother Rebecca's back. I slammed my palm against the curb and scraped it against the cement until I bled.

The next day, I found the marble whale under the *flamboyán* tree. The whale was hidden in the grass. I took it back to the house. It was heavier than I'd expected. Dad was home from work and stood in the kitchen, making himself a drink.

I said, "You forgot this. You just left it out there."

"Where did you find that?" He put down the drink. He took the whale out of my arms.

"Near the pool."

When Mom saw the whale, she grabbed my arm. I said, "What are you doing?"

Dad said, "Julia, I told you to bring that in the house. How could you leave it for the kids to find?"

"That whale always did upset me," Mom said. She was hurting my arm.

I sensed she was afraid of Dad. So she'd turned the talk to herself. I was trying to learn that trick. I whispered to her, "Nanny took the whale in the pool."

She dropped my wrist. "No, she didn't," Mom said. She began combing my hair with her perfumed fingers. "Yes, she did, Clarissa, but you mustn't tell Cora or Michael. You mustn't tell anyone. Promise me?" Then Mom turned to Dad and said, "To-

Mother's Bootstrap

After my grandmother's death, my father spent more time at the office. When he came home, he talked to us about Operation Bootstrap. Sometimes he read us government ads in *The New York Times*: the island had many mountains, impressive weather, low wages. The ads showed Governor Muñoz Marín's photograph. Sometimes he read us articles written by professors: Bootstrap was an appropriation of America's economic highs and lows. He said we should hear both sides.

We knew the technical points. My father's stores were retail. He wasn't on the island for the tax exemption. He was there for the slow upheaval: he told us that our family, our Isla, helped Fomento, the economic development agency, to succeed. His business and politics were our bedtime stories.

*   *   *

The tenth-anniversary party of Isla was at our country club, on the northwest coast near Fajardo. I was about to turn ten, too. A Rockefeller owned the club. We stayed in a large white *cabaña* surrounded by palm trees and near the beach. Aunt Nadia, her husband, Stuart, and their children, Thaddeus and Ann, were all staying next door. They lived in the city of Santurce and had driven to the club that morning.

It was still light out when Dad took us to the stone plantation house where the party was to be. We were to meet Aunt Nadia and Uncle Stuart at the house. It had a restaurant upstairs. A large lawn with a pool lay in front. An Australian pine tree shed its small cones all over the grass; a West Indies palm towered over a yellow tent. There was a stage made of wooden planks, covered with palm leaves, and a podium made of bamboo branches. Behind the stage and the tent I could see the ocean.

Cora and I wandered into the tent. Inside, Cousin Ann was whispering to Cousin Thaddeus. They looked alike, both with dark curly hair and with Aunt Nadia's pale eyes. Ann was seven, a year older than Cora. Thaddeus was eight. They both had Uncle Stuart's thin face, which made them appear always a little hungry.

"The band's going to be good," Ann said. "Why don't you play the piano, Clarissa?"

I said, "Why doesn't Thaddeus play the violin?"

"I'm going to burn my violin," Thaddeus told his sister.

Ann showed us a photograph of her Brownie group. "I'll be a Girl Scout soon."

"My mom says Girl Scouts are Barbie dolls," Cora said.

"Your mother doesn't know anything about America," Ann said. She left to find her father.

On the long buffet table, hibiscus flowers floated in white bowls between platters of shrimps and scallops, caviar and salmon, cheese and bread. I took some brie. A chef was carving a roast of beef. Cora pointed to the end of the beef. The chef peered down at her through round glasses. Cora said, "I know 'If' by Rudyard Kipling. I don't like nursery rhymes. My daddy says they're too silly for little girls." She laughed. The chef sliced her some well-done roast beef.

Dad stood by the entrance to the tent. He lit a cigarette for

Mrs. Please. Her husband was the head of a chemical plant. Once, he'd arranged for our class to tour the plant. He'd given me a kiss in front of my friends.

Mrs. Please had a drawl. "The last time I saw you was at the Variety Club screening last year," she said to me. "We saw *My Fair Lady*." With her napkin she wiped lipstick off the rim of her glass. "Oh, David, where are the days when films just oozed with genius? Remember Huston's *The Treasure of the Sierra Madre*—"

"Or *The Trouble With Harry*, with MacLaine," Dad said.

She said, "Your Julia reminds me of Shirley MacLaine."

"Julia has her own style. No one comes close to it," he said. He waved to Aunt Nadia.

Aunt Nadia's step was light. She looked as if she were hurrying through shallow water. Her dark hair was loose and shining. She hugged Dad and then described to Mrs. Please a new shoe store on Ashford Avenue. Aunt Nadia said she loved their advertising campaign: it was very European.

Uncle Stuart danced over. His gray hair seemed whiter than when I'd last seen him. He'd splattered wine on the bottom of his tie. He said, "Michael's getting so big, he's almost the size of Thaddeus."

"Stuart, did you get those papers I sent you last week?" Dad said. "How's Torres working out at the Fajardo store?"

"We'll discuss it over lunch on Monday," Uncle Stuart said. He threw Michael in the air.

My mother once told me she disapproved of Aunt Nadia's weapons in marriage. "Our temperaments choose our arms, Clarissa—those guns and knives that help us defend our sides of a contract." My mother's arms were wit and eccentricity. Aunt Nadia's were strategies and rebuttals. My mother distrusted them. She led me to believe that Aunt Nadia ran Uncle Stuart's job as vice president of Isla. She told me Aunt Nadia "swore" to improve him.

My father praised Aunt Nadia as director of advertising at Isla. But he also told me that no one should weaken another person the way Nadia weakens Stuart. She'd married Uncle Stuart in 1956. He'd been an interior designer for a small firm that serviced churches, schools and prisons.

*   *   *

The band began playing what sounded like a waltz. It was dark.
Aunt Nadia was dancing with a man named Eric Melon. Melon
leered at her bustline. They passed Cora and me. Eric Melon
made Aunt Nadia do a turn. She faced us and said, "Smile, girls.
You're our two little hostesses."

Cora and I didn't answer. We sat on a rock near the pool.
Tiny frogs chirped the sound of their name: co-quí. By the trees,
the *coquís* were singing louder and faster.

"See that lady?" Cora said. She pointed to a young woman
whose black hair framed her face like a hood. "I don't like her. She
went up to Dad and kissed him, like a long time. She's with that
man, see?" Cora pointed to a man with mustard hair as short as
a soldier's. He stood in front of the tent, watching the dancers. He
wore a white tuxedo. "Well, that guy, he's a photographer."

"How do you know?" I said.

"I talked to him."

"You talk to everyone you see."

"He has this huge camera," she said. "It's on that chair."

"Stop pointing," I told her. "It's not polite."

The young woman was flirting with Dad. Mom and Dad never
flirted. They were married, I thought; they didn't have to. But
Aunt Nadia kissed Uncle Stuart's cheek.

"Come on." I took Cora's hand.

We rushed up to Dad and I said, "Cora wants to dance."

"In a minute. The next dance is for you," he said. "Cora,
Clarissa, this is Anna-Marie Benton."

Cora said, "Let's dance this dance."

Anna-Marie Benton placed her hand on Cora's shoulder. "I've
been overthrown. See you later, David."

"Overthrown?" Dad said. "You?"

The Labor Committee gave out the awards for best management.
Dad won two. At the podium he accepted the trophies. They
had a gold-plated *coquí* sitting on a palm tree. He said thank you
and Aunt Nadia gave the speech. She talked about Isla as a

family. She made a toast in Russian. Her Russian wasn't good; she spoke it whenever she drank a lot.

Mom said to Dad, "Yes, it sounds rather nice, but what does it mean? Speaking so no one understands . . ."

Anna-Marie Benton adjusted a diamond earring in her left ear. She said, "Julia, it only has to *sound* good."

Mom whispered to me, "Don't talk to that Anna-Marie, love. She's a tart."

"A what?"

"You heard what I said."

I was standing next to the guitarist, listening to his chords. He led the band into the merengue. Anna-Marie Benton was dancing with Dad.

Mom's body swayed to the beat. She sipped champagne. She sucked in her cheeks after each sip. Some of her hair had fallen out of her bun. Suddenly she shouted, "Look, Nadia." And she dropped her empty glass. She stepped on it. I heard the glass splinter. "That's for good luck," she said. "Remember, Stuart, at my wedding, when David missed the glass? So, there, I've made up for it."

I was looking for Cora so we could leave. I found her on the second floor of the plantation house. She was eating an éclair with her hands. The tables had candles on them but no silverware. The chef sat beside Cora, drinking a beer.

I said, "Come on, time to go."

The chef cleaned his eyeglasses with a napkin.

"We had very delicious cake," Cora said.

I thanked the chef and took Cora away. I said, "Why are you bothering him?"

"He asked me if I wanted cake. And he loves the *coquís*, too. He told me they won't sing anywhere but Puerto Rico. Did you know that? They die if they go to another island. Know what else? He says there are too many Americans here. But we're American, aren't we?"

I didn't answer her. I thought of Mom breaking the glass. I thought of Dad dancing with Anna-Marie Benton.

We ran into Aunt Nadia downstairs. Her face was flushed. She said, "Why not drink to your mother?" But she didn't lift her glass. She walked away.

Lanterns stood along the path to the *cabañas*. Mom held her shoes in her hands. The back of her gown was dragging on the ground. She said to Dad, "You have no sense of humor."

"The kind of joke only you get," he said. He was carrying Michael in his arms.

"It's all right for you and Nadia to have your fun, but it's not all right for me. Is that it, David?"

"That's it," Dad said.

On the way home the next day, Dad was hunched over the wheel. "It's coming up on the left. See it?" He tapped his window and pointed to a new pharmaceutical plant.

"You call this saving the island?" Mom said. "Cutting down trees and putting up concrete boxes?"

"Julia, it's amazing how well Bootstrap's working. I'd say there must be fifteen hundred factories here by now."

He pulled into the driveway of the plant. The building was white, long and low. Plastic shutters gleamed in the sunlight. Men were sawing pale wood in a yard. Dad started the car again. We passed a housing project. All the apartments were pastel and oblong, like miniature factories. Women in pink curlers leaned on the cement balconies.

Cora said, "Why's it called Operation Bootstrap, again?"

"You need to keep your boots on to get anything done," Dad said. "A man's weak without his shoes."

"Look, Isla, Isla!" Michael was shouting.

A new store stood near the housing project. The letters were blue and bold. Shopping carts were chained to a pole.

Mom said, "Look at all this construction. It'll cause some good old pollution, that's what it'll do. Why do Americans always think they're the answer to everything? People like you think you're the answer." She half closed her eyes.

Dad shook his head. He bit off the end of his cigar. "I can't have this discussion with you."

"But why go changing everything?" she said, her voice softer. "It's so pretty as it is." She took out a cigarette and then opened the window.

Dad said, "People were starving."

"Yes," Mom said, turning to us. "Tell your father how we all know about starving."

Equator

I was equatorial. Being between Clarissa and Michael made me whimsical, adventurous and needless to say, refulgent, until the day my body pulled its trick. Now I choose to retire into the background. A few good yards between me and another help keep my sanity.

This month, December 1980, Clarissa will be twenty-five. She isn't the kind to talk about her birthday; she refuses to celebrate it. I sent her a gift early: an onyx box for her oodles of earrings and rings. On occasion I can be self-absorbed. With my sister and brother I try never to be.

"This time," Clarissa said, "this time, I'm not going to the hospital. Let Mom see I won't give in." She struck at the keys. God, she was invincible. I thought we were so unlike one another, so unlike two sister eggs hatched by the same torrid-bellied hen. I was tiny at age eight and weighed fifty-two. She was twelve. She was tall. While I thrived on spice—the hottest, plumpest peppers—she ate the most sugary fruits. Everything of mine, the blond hair (how pale), the blue eyes (how sensitive), everything, down to the metatarsals that broke when I ran barefoot, I wanted to disown. I wanted her eyes—murky green, slanting up a bit. I wanted her emerging breasts, her long legs, her wavy hair. I said, Come on, let's switch bodies.

Clarissa said, patting my hand, "We need you just as you are." Suddenly she cursed: Coño. She rested an elegant pinkie on the last key of the Pianola. At the school piano, she found full breath. Free-dom, she'd say. This Pianola was a frustration to her, I knew that, yet when Father or Mother slipped in a roll of music and they sang together, Clarissa's eyes always brightened.

When I was six, she'd taught me the proper role of sister: backup. We had our routine: she played the melody and I was the chorus. I dutifully sang—blue, gray, red—each color matching a note. I laughed. Threw the old head back, shook the shoulders (a bit learned from Father) and stomped the left foot. By the time I was seven, I'd learned every note: B sharp was lizard green; B flat was lime. If I hesitated, oh, she'd get impatient, foot pumping the pedal. Sometimes she'd hit me. I had to squeal. I'd say to Father: Clarissa punched me. When very mad, she'd slam me in the stomach with two fists. I bent over and whimpered, thinking: This is what it feels like to go. So I once told her, You're making me feel as if I'm dying. She said, I couldn't kill you, don't be ridiculous, you're my sistah.

I knew I was about to upset her. I said quietly, "Mom wants us ready by five."

"I won't see another baby," she said, hitting the piano bench with her hand. "Last month it was Missus Alvarez, the month before Missus Poe. It's amazing Mom gets away with it."

But Mother was determined to get her way; she loved to go into a hospital room, impeccably dressed in a suit made by a local seamstress. She'd bring gifts. She'd hand over a little treasure for a stranger's newborn, introducing herself as Mrs. Julia Lyon. Some women knew us; they were old friends. Some women pretended they knew us, and some disrupted Mother's pattern:

once or twice we'd been forced to leave. Mrs. Spare, our garru-
lous neighbor, called Mother Saint Julia.

Clarissa had once asked Mother, "What's the point of all these
visits?"

She replied, putting pressure on the small of my sister's back so
she'd stand up straight, "What a mother does isn't strictly by
intuition. By visiting different mothers we may decide for ourselves the course of action that works best for our own children."

Clarissa said, "But what if I'm never a mother?"

Now she was playing an A flat again and again as she asked
me, "Don't you see there's something really weird with all this,
with her?"

I jumped off the piano bench. "She's always kind." I was proud
of Mother; I admired her generosity.

"Cora, you're just as weird as she is. I'm sleeping at María's
tonight."

What a day it was, beastly enough to exterminate *coquís*, crickets
and *reinitas*. Ninety-nine degrees at 6:00 A.M., and by noon, one
hundred and two. No wind; leaves shriveling on branches; moths
and butterflies carpeting our terrace.

In this heat, Mother was taking us to see Faith Samson, a
friend of the Spares'. How much of a friend, Mother wasn't too
sure. She'd overheard Maggie, the Spares' housekeeper, talk
about a Faith Samson and a baby who had felt like a cactus when
coming out.

The hospital, next to the fort of El Morro, looked like a
run-down colonial house. There were three *pastelillo* stands in
the parking lot. I loved *pastelillos*: the crispiness of the fried
dough, the heaviness of the stuffing, whether cheese or meat. I
wanted one, but Mother forbade us to eat them. We got out of
the car. Several men were buying sodas at one stand; the vendor
was singing. Feigning invincibility from the heat, I also started to
sing: *We don't have to march like the infantry, Shoot like the artillery,
Ride like the cavalry, We don't have to zoom over Germany, 'Cause
we're in the Signal Corps—Amphibious!* Uncle Stuart had taught
me that tune.

Michael walked slowly. Whatever he was told, he'd do. When he obeyed unwillingly, his eyes darkened, as they did today. "What'd you buy?" he asked Mother.

"A music box. They had a little girl. Now, what did I say the mum's name was?" She groped in her deep bag, looking for the gift, and fished out a compact, a change purse, a handkerchief, a tiny troll I'd given her.

"You said her name was Faith Samson," I told her.

Michael told her, "And you said the baby was a boy."

And Mother said, "We'll be just fine without your sister."

Faith Samson's room was in the west hall of the maternity ward. Women, with their bellies exposed, were lingering in the long hall, one woman noisily fanning herself with a newspaper. I'd never seen so many women all at once in bras and slips. The walls smelled of grease. Through an open door, I watched a nurse carefully putting ice cubes on the forehead of a woman.

Before going into Faith Samson's room, Mother brushed my hair. She tried to brush Michael's, but he stepped back, and she stroked at nothing. We hesitated at the open door. In Faith Samson's room, a bunch of daisies stood in a large paper cup. An old black man rocked gently in a straight chair. One eye was sealed tight. His lower lip drooped a bit. Was he drooling or about to speak? Neither. His good eye took us in.

"Is this Faith Samson's room?" Mother said.

"Uhum," the man grunted.

Faith Samson looked like a woman from an illustration in my mythology book: her long black hair was straight and fell onto the sheets. She had olive skin and wore orange-red lipstick. But she wasn't much older than Clarissa. I was so shocked that I blushed. I'd never seen a teenage mother before.

"Yes?" Faith Samson said and barely moved.

"I'm Missus Julia Lyon," Mother said, "and these are my children."

Who wanted to be her child right then? I wanted to be an orderly or a nurse who happened to have stumbled into the room. Faith Samson was way too young to be a mother. I schemed with invisible rage: how could we leave? At the same time, I couldn't stop staring at Faith Samson's face. The longer

I looked the more beautiful she became to me. Michael was also staring.

Mother said, "We were visiting a friend in the neighborhood, and Missus Spare told me you just had a baby boy. Congratulations! Here you go, my pretty love, a little gift for your angel."

"Who's these people," the man said. He cracked his neck and then fumbled in his inside jacket pocket for a pack of cigarettes. There were stains of perspiration under his arms. Why not take off his jacket? I thought. He lit a match and snuffed it between his thick fingers.

Mother said, "Sir, please don't smoke. It's not good for the mum. Honestly, sir, I know how you feel. I'm a smoker myself, but never, I'd never light up before a new mum."

The man smoked. Michael shuffled his sneakers against the yellow linoleum floor.

"These people are friends of Maggie's, I guess," Faith Samson said to the old man. "You know Maggie, Pa. She works for the Spares, the people in the gray house in Santa María. I seen you at the Spares'," she said to me.

Mother sat down and violently waved the smoke away from Faith Samson. Michael turned the fan so the smoke slipped out the window.

"Why'd you come see me?" Faith Samson said.

Mother flashed her wide smile. "To celebrate! It's all so wonderful. Faith . . . may I call you Faith? Please, I'm Julia. You should have seen me with my middle one." She pulled me to her side. "All that pain for such a little thing. But then you have this darling child, and isn't . . . isn't it all so wonderful? I'm so happy you look so fine."

To me, Faith Samson seemed tired, weak, not fine at all.

The old man put his swollen hands on his hips, cigarette smoking in his mouth, and said, "So what you doing here?"

"Excuse me?" Mother blushed and played with the folds of her skirt.

"He wants to know what we're doing here," I said, thinking Clarissa was right not to come.

"That's my father," Faith Samson said. She took the gift from the table and opened it. It was a pink music box. She lifted the lid and a ballerina popped up and twirled for a few seconds to a lullaby. Faith Samson giggled and said it was sweet.

Mr. Samson's bones clicked as he crept over to the bed. He snatched the music box from his daughter, wound it, placed it on the windowsill and writhed back into his former position. He said, "I had a girl once who had one of them toys. She was curvy and nice."

"The music puts you to sleep," Michael said.

Faith Samson told him that after her baby fell asleep, she'd listen to the music box until she was asleep.

Mother asked Mr. Samson, "Would you be kind enough to show me the little boy?"

Mr. Samson stayed quiet and sucked, like a child, on his bloated lower lip. When the music stopped, he got up again, still making that clicking sound, to rewind the box.

Mother clapped her hands once and said to Faith Samson, "Well, then, you know what babies love? They love when you sing: *Around the corner and under the trees, There was a baby named . . .*"

"Named Adam," Faith Samson said.

A nurse hurried into the room. She tapped her watch and told us, "*Bendito*. Visitors are supposed to leave." Then the nurse recognized Mother, kissed her and made her an offering: Would Mrs. Lyon like to see the baby?

"You go and take it easy with my Faith's baby," Mr. Samson said to the nurse. He approached Mother, seated on the bed, her hat perched on her lap, and told her, "I've seen nurses drop babies like they was gum. Babies have big souls. They're much heavier than you think." He sounded harsh.

Mother smiled and said, "Certainly that's what a father does best: he's strong enough to carry a—"

"I doan see no father," Mr. Samson said. His bad eye twitched.

That night, at home, Father was watching television in the den. Clarissa had gone to sleep at her friend María's house. Michael sat on the floor and pulled a model airplane box out from under the couch. Mother asked me and Father if we wanted anything,

anything at all. I imagined pinning her down as if she were Gulliver. I sat on Father's lap. A commercial for *Goya* beans, on sale at Isla, came on the screen.

Father said, his voice raspy from a cigar, "Julia, do me a favor. Don't go to the hospital anymore. I got a call late this afternoon from a Mister Abraham Samson."

"I knew he was a troublemaker," Mother said, sitting at the edge of Father's ottoman. "How dare he call you! Who does this Mister Samson think he is?" She stood. "He's one troublemaker is what he is."

Father said, "I'm asking you not to go to the hospital anymore."

I thought: Do Dad a small favor, Mum. Listen to him.

Michael gave up on his model, grabbed the newspaper, tore out a page and made a wide-winged airplane. He sent it flying, but it tumbled and dove.

Mother said to Father, "I feel for this Faith. She's very young and quite alone. My mum died when I was young, too young. I know how scared this Faith is." She picked up the paper airplane and then rested her hand on Father's chair.

I said, "Maybe she's not alone. Maybe she has a sister or a brother."

"I just phoned Farrah Spare and she says Faith has no one but that Mister Samson," Mother told me.

Father said, his eyes on the screen, "It's hot for visits. Stop going, Julia." He raised his hand and let it fall on hers. "I'll go sweep the porch."

"Lots of dead things out there," Michael said and gathered all the tiny airplane parts, to shove them into the box. "I'll help."

After they left the den, Mother told me excitedly, "He was not a kind man, that Mister Samson. I sensed it. Imagine not having a soul in the world but an unkind man like that."

I'd made up my mind: I wanted to help Father, too. I'd stop Mother from going to the hospital again. "Mom."

She came over to me, tucked in the back of my pajama top, turned me around and lightly patted my stomach. "Yes, love?"

Oh, I couldn't be like my sister. How could I defy Mother? But hadn't I already seen enough moaning and perspiring women? I said, "Mom, I don't want to see any more babies."

"You and your sister! It's dreadful the way you two walk away when people need help. That's because you both have everything you need. When I was a child, there was a war. And we had no money. Nothing like this," she said, pointing to the furniture and paintings as if I'd never seen them before. "You don't know how it can be. And you'll never have to know, God willing." She told me I was getting big enough to give her trouble. Then she turned off the television and said, "Cora, doesn't Clarissa like her own bed?"

"I guess she does."

"Then why must she hop from house to house, sleeping over at the homes of her friends? Don't you ever forget, young lady, you've only one family."

Papayas,
Filets

Mom hired Faith Samson to help Rosa. I'd never met Faith Samson before. Michael said Faith was young. Cora said Faith's father was black. To me, Faith looked white. Her skin was smooth and olive-toned. She told me she was from Trinidad. She'd come to Puerto Rico as a child. Her son, Adam, wasn't as dark as she. Faith left Adam in the guest room, and Mom watched the baby. Rosa complained about his crying to Mom. Rosa complained about Faith to us.

Faith cleaned the house differently from Rosa. She liked to saturate a rag with furniture polish. She then roped the rag to the head of the vacuum cleaner. With the vacuum cleaner, she reached under the living room table to polish and vacuum the floor. Cora, Michael and I were watching her from the kitchen. Rosa wasn't watching. She handed a chunk of papaya to each of us. Papaya juice ran down Cora's chin.

Faith was soon finished. She joined us in the kitchen. She

held up a piece of papaya. "You don't know how good a papaya can be until you see how I make one," she said to Michael. She called him "a bold boy."

Cora said, "What do you mean?"

"I'll show you," Faith said. She took a papaya. She cut it into four star-like shapes.

"*Qué niña*," Rosa said. "It's food, it's no picture."

It was Faith's third day. She was arranging her melon stars and flowers on one of Mom's silver platters. She dabbed each piece with fresh cream laced with Amaretto. Rosa later discovered there was a liqueur in the cream. She threw the fruit out. She said we were too young for liqueur. Faith apologized. But she couldn't understand why Rosa was mad. She whispered to me, "Clarissa, was Rosa once a drinker? Tell me—did she like to drink?" I said Rosa never drank. I didn't care one way or another about Faith.

That evening, Dad and Mom went out to a Chaîne des Rôtisseurs dinner. Dad had been a member of the gourmet club for years. Rosa sat with us in the den. We watched an old movie in Spanish: a revenge story called *El Paso Malo*. A woman finds out her husband has been unfaithful while journeying to find gold. She sets out to steal his gold. In the end, both the man and the woman get killed by poisonous snakes.

Rosa made us chocolate malteds. She insisted on getting us blankets. When she returned, she'd missed important scenes in the movie. We all tried to fill her in and then we missed parts of the movie. She laughed. She had this hilly laugh that got loud and then soft, one minute to the next. She was one of the few people who made me feel as if talking to her were the best time she could have.

After the movie, the news came on. Rosa said, "I don't like the news anymore. And there's nothing good about Peru."

Cora curled up and rested her head on my lap. She said to Rosa, "Tell us a story, please."

"Michael, in bed and I'll tell you stories," Rosa said. She tapped Michael on the shoulder.

"Not fair," he said.

We hurried to his room.

Rosa sat on the bed. I gave her a pillow. Cora lay down next to Michael.

Rosa said, "After my mother's first husband died, before I came into the world, my mother, Junia—"

"Junia was her name?" Michael said.

"She worked in a cotton factory, making sweaters. She was lucky to work."

"When did you come to America?" I said.

"Wait, wait. . . . My mother got tired of working for so little, so she moved to Lima, where the money was better. In Lima, which was very beautiful then, *muy linda,* she was a cook for a banker. And one night, she met a man who worked on a guano boat—"

"What's guano?" Cora said.

"From birds, to make the soil good—*cómo se dice en inglés . . . ?*

"Fertilizer," I said. "Guano's to make the soil rich."

"Yes, *mamita.* So this man, Juan Manuel, was my father. Oh, I forget him sometimes. My mother moved with him to Callao, a town on the sea near Lima. And soon she was pregnant with me. But what I really remember about my father was that he always talked about the wonders of America."

Cora said, "I think the islands are wonderful."

"Many places are wonderful," Rosa said. "Callao was nice because the boats stopped there. I liked it. I helped my mother make sweaters for tourists. Then, when I was fourteen, my father went on a train to Arequipa. He was going to meet a man about a new business. Guano was no good anymore. *El Niño*—the bad weather—made the ocean change currents, and there was no more food for the bird that made the guano. But the train was in an accident and my father was killed. My mother didn't cry. She just rushed to the hospital with clean clothes for him. She said he had to look handsome. In Peru, it is very important to respect the dead."

"She changed his clothes when he was dead?" Michael said.

I worried he'd have nightmares. I stroked his hair the way Mom would.

Rosa raised her hands and said, "And then my mother stopped eating."

"She starved herself?" Cora leaned closer to her.

"And she had dreams: people stealing her things," Rosa said. "So she locked everything. When I had to get something, even bread, I had to unlock a big lock. And the locks were big. You needed big keys. She kept the keys under the bed in a flour sack." From her pocket, she took out her rosary beads. She kissed them. For her mother, I thought.

"When I was twenty-eight years old, I was a cleaning girl for a college in Callao. I stayed there until my mother died. I remember I sold all the locks and keys and all the furniture. I got a lot of money and came to Puerto Rico. Here I worked for Helen Meyer, very sweet, for many years. And I met Martín, and now he's—" She stopped as if to remember something. "*Bien guapo,*" Rosa said and laughed. "But he's dead now for many years. Doña Helen is dead, too."

Michael was almost sleeping.

Cora said, "Take us to Peru, Rosa."

I pictured unlocking a bread cupboard to get bread. I wondered if Junia hadn't trusted her own daughter.

We were at the dinner table. Dad was talking about flying to Chicago for the Food Marketing Institute convention.

Mom said, "I can't leave the children. It's a bad time for me to go." She pursed her lips and tapped them with her forefinger.

"Why use them as an excuse?" Dad said.

"Smells good," Cora said. She slumped in her chair.

Rosa came out, holding a platter. She'd cut the filet mignons into odd shapes. Broccoli stalks sprouted from the middle of each piece of meat. The stalks had lines etched in them, which made them look rotten. She'd cut the potatoes into the shape of fish. Rosa set the platter in the center of the table. She wiped her hands on her white apron. She then sprinkled salt and pepper on the platter. "*Está lloviendo,*" she said.

"It is not raining! Rosa, what have you done?" Mom said. She covered her cheeks with her hands.

"What a surprise, what a nice surprise," Dad said, "You've been busy in the kitchen, haven't you?"

I said, "Are they islands or . . . ?" It hurt me to see Mom getting mad at Rosa.

"The meat is the island. Here are the trees," she said, pointing to the broccoli. "And here are the fish."

Cora looked at me and said, "I like it."

"I'd like to know what's happened with our dinner," Mom said. "These are very expensive cuts. What has happened to them?"

"They are still good, Doña Julia . . . ," Rosa said.

"She's just doing the same thing Faith does," Michael told Mom.

Mom gripped Rosa by the shoulders. She said, "Are you upset over Faith? I hired her to help you."

"Oh, Doña Julia, I don't need any help."

"I didn't know," Mom said. She sat back down and looked at Dad.

I thought: How could she know? Lately, she didn't really know how Michael, Cora and I were doing. She spent all her time with Faith's baby.

Dad said, "Rosa, it's all great, just great." He helped himself to some meat.

Lemur

"There's Saint Croix, Michael, see?"

"Yes," I said, squinting to spot the land.

You'd been telling me all about how you and Aunt Nadia had started Isla. You rested your right foot against the lower rail and locked your hands behind your back. It was our last boat trip together. Remember, Father? I was eleven and I remember a lot: how the wind made your shorts and shirt flap against your body and your rippled hair flatten against your scalp. I was sitting behind you in the swivel chair, the steering wheel and controls before me. We were in the tower, and I could hear Clarissa, Cora and Mother moving around on the boat below us.

Mother wouldn't take the boat from Puerto Rico to Saint John but agreed to fly to Saint Thomas and get on the boat at Red Hook. We'd spent the night at a hotel in Charlotte Amalie and left Saint Thomas in the morning, the current moving with us.

The boat, *Justicia,* was forty feet long, and we were going to be at sea for two nights.

From the bow, Clarissa shouted, "David!"

You said, saluting her, "Be there in a few seconds."

When Clarissa was mad at you, she liked to use your first name. Days before we'd left Puerto Rico, she'd told you she wanted to stop her piano lessons. And you'd said, Why don't you know what the hell you're doing? Later, she'd said to me, Our father is an unfair man.

"We're speeding up," I told you. "Do you feel it?"

"This toy flies over water. That's why it costs a pretty penny. . . ." You were still watching Clarissa as she carefully stepped near the rail to get to the stern. You said to me, "Now, where was I?"

"You and Aunt Nadia asked Nanny for money—"

"Right! And Nanny goes into the spare room and comes back with a key. Then we're all marching up to the attic, and out of a broken music box, Nanny pulls fifty-five hundred-dollar bills. And that's the money that helped us open the Santurce store. Remember we're talking '54."

My first memory, July 1962; the fourth store; we're in Fajardo. There's Uncle Stuart, Aunt Nadia, and right next to me, there's the mayor, María Socorro Pérez. Mother, holding my hand and looking proud, stands by Mayor Pérez. I'm just two. You hand me a pair of scissors and I reach up. Quick snip of the ribbon. You shout: *That's my son! Where's the champagne?* The cold champagne pouring over me.

"Who snipped the ribbon on your first opening day?" I said.

"Your grandmother, of course. And what a crowd . . . ! We were home free." You sat on the bench and beckoned me to sit next to you. "Nonetheless, you must always be prepared for a disaster. And you must trust your instinct. When you're in the business, you'll see that."

Río, the captain's hand, was making us lunch. I thought Río was cool: he had dark skin and his ear had been bitten off the year before by a man who'd tried to mug him. In return, Río had rammed his head into the man's stomach, making the man collapse on the street and gasp.

You climbed down from the tower first and I saw how you were beginning to lose your hair. As I went down, I watched Mother's shadow move under the canopy that stretched over the stern. Mother, wearing a blue cotton hat and a loose shift printed with blue flowers, was setting the table. She had her white skin coated with suntan lotion and was barefoot, her bunions shiny and pink. She almost always wore shoes, even on sand, and looking at her feet, I remembered being five years old and sick with the mumps: Mother reading to me, lying beside me so her bare foot wriggled next to my cheek. I rubbed her foot but skipped over the bunion. What's this? I'd asked, and she'd said, That is a sign of intelligence.

She put six plastic glasses into the holes in the table and in the center hole set the bottle of wine. Wine was your water; Clarissa was allowed one glass. At first Mother had protested—Clarissa was only sixteen—but you ignored her and said, Better to develop the taste buds early on.

"David," Clarissa said, "please open the wine. The cork's stuck."

"I hate it when you call Dad David," Cora said. She sat down and brushed the suntan lotion grease from her arms onto the chair.

"Don't hate," you said to Cora and then tasted the wine, which you described as "*magnífico.*" Holding up the glass, you turned to Mother. "Wouldn't it be nice to have a place of our own to get away to?"

"A clean place would be nice, a place without factories or cars," Mother said, "and, yes, without a supermarket."

You sipped the wine and looked away from Mother. I tried to think of an island where you didn't have a store, but I couldn't.

The captain came out, singing a song about how blue the sky was. His name was Alfonso Menudo. He was one of your better friends, a distributor of your best-selling brand of pasta. He had a cleft in his chin and liked to laugh a lot. He reached for the platter of bread and chose the two largest pieces.

Río, his long curly hair like a Rastafarian's, carried out a platter from the galley. He'd made shrimp with garlic sauce, sautéed quickly, the smell of garlic still swirling in the breeze, hanging over us like one of Mother's big hats.

The captain started serving and I noticed he had on a ruby ring that covered a third of his thick finger. "Where's that from?" I pointed to the ruby.

"The Grenadines. I met a woman there as big as myself and she had three rings. A ruby, a diamond and, on her pinkie, an emerald. I bought the ruby. But it took us three goddamn days to get the ring off her finger. She stayed in the bath for three days. Then I stayed with the woman. Her name was Pearl."

"I've never known anyone named Pearl," I said.

"Ah, Michael, Michael, you're one to fool," he said and laughed, his big hand covering the ring. "The ring was my father's, God rest his sinful soul. . . ."

"This trip is a real pleasure, Alfonso," you said. "I'm having such a good time I'm thinking that maybe I need a retreat of my own."

"I knew a guy who had a house on the island of Mykonos. He'd go there for months at a time. He'd never say he was just going away. He'd say he was 'vanishing,' " the captain said, opening up his hands as if to show they were empty.

"The Mediterranean, the Caribbean . . . the distance doesn't matter. I'm talking about a place where a man and his family can be on their own time, the way you are with your boat," you said without smiling. "Julia, dear, where'd you pack my book?"

"I put both our books in the gray bag," Mother said.

"What gray bag?" you said, scratching your forehead. You looked over your shoulder and took a Mets baseball hat from the top of the cooler and you put it on. "You're telling me I don't have a book."

The captain assured us he had a whole library in the cabin, and anything we wanted to read, we should just take. Cora asked for *Robinson Crusoe*.

The captain said to me, "We'll be at Saint John any minute. Why don't we put you at the wheel? You'll anchor us."

After lunch, I went up to the tower and waited. When we

were close to shore, the captain dropped the anchor, and I put the boat in forward, slowly, then I put the boat in reverse.

"Are we anchored, mate?" the captain shouted from the bow.

"I think so," I said, my voice shaky. I wanted to show you I could do this; you were always telling me I was too quiet: I should do more, make myself known. The anchor seemed to hold. I felt I was blushing, but how could I be blushing after my success, the anchor no longer visible? I put the boat in neutral, climbed down the ladder, went into my cabin again to take my shirt off and then I felt the boat moving again. I hurried out of the cabin and to the stern in time to see the anchor rip through the water.

You said to me, "Next time you'll have to make the anchor catch."

Cora lounged on the bow, wearing almost nothing. Her bikini at its widest was three inches, permitting me to see a tit. She outlined her nose with her forefinger, let her finger slip down to her mouth, her neck, her bathing suit top. She adjusted the top. There, no more tit. Flat tits. Not like Teresa. Kissed me in the playground. Please, just one kiss, Michael, and I did.

"I like it here. Do you?" Cora asked.

"I'm going to live here one day."

To the north, Jost Van Dyke; to the west, Saint Thomas. We were in a small bay, at a private beach. The captain knew the owner, an eccentric hermit called Old Kaiser, and the captain had told us, Very few boats are allowed to anchor here. The water was protected, warm, turquoise, transparent, and Clarissa was in it, swimming to shore. Cora said, "Come on, let's go to the beach."

She got to the beach before me and I could hear her trying to catch her breath when I got to the sand. She'd gone too fast, the swim having sucked color from her cheeks. She rested her cheek against the sand and said, "Oh, this feels good."

We strolled along the beach, our feet in the water. Inland, clusters of palm trees sent shadows across the beach and two brown hills rose above the trees. Beyond the palms, ferns and

some calabash trees appeared to be huddling, with their huge
fruits hanging. We couldn't find Clarissa, so we wandered back
to where the captain stood pitching the canopy. Río pounded
the last stake into the ground while the captain rolled down
mosquito nets from folds in the top of the canopy. You sat in a
portable lounge chair with a book. Mother rested in a matching
lounge chair, her hands on her stomach. The dinghy was on the
beach.

Cora wanted to know what you were reading. You showed her
the title: *The Insect Society.* "What a library our friend Alfonso
has!" you said. "It's all science."

The captain threw Cora a book called *The Anatomy of the
Arachnid.* "Best of its kind," he told her while setting up a white
plastic table.

Then Clarissa sauntered into view and said she'd spotted an
abandoned house on the other side of the beach.

"That was a customhouse," the captain said. "But don't go
over the hill. We don't want to disturb Old Kaiser." He rode the
dinghy to the boat, returning with two large covered trays, a big
cooler and a long basket. He peeled the cellophane off one tray
and uncovered roast beef and turkey and cheese. He pulled from
the cooler a bottle of champagne, one of wine and two bottles of
mineral water. "We had such a big lunch," he said. "I thought
we'd take it easy for dinner."

We ate quickly. As we were finishing, a yacht came into sight.
It was larger than *Justicia* and yellow lights illuminated the upper
and lower decks. There were two red dinghies hanging on either
side of the yacht.

"I'll be damned. Mitchell Willet," the captain said.

You said, "The Willet of Banco del Mundo?"

"You got it, Davy. I heard his wife just passed away and he
took it bad. It looks like he's here for the night.

Mother held up her water and said, "There goes our privacy."

Mitchell Willet was balding; the top of his head had flakes of
curling dead skin burned from the sun. He looked about fifty and
was small and his brown eyes bulged a little, but otherwise his

features were almost pretty. Every once in a while, as if he couldn't keep up an act anymore, he lapsed into Spanish. He said, "I've been feeling poorly lately. I'm off to Martinique in the morning for a long, good rest." In his white sailor pants and white moccasins, he looked healthy, but his voice was as worn as someone's on an old record. While he lit a cigarette, I was wondering why he stayed with us if he didn't want company.

Mary Point, a stretch of land that protected the bay, blocked the wind, which, the captain pointed out, was unfortunate at night, as the mosquitoes seemed to burst out of pockets in the air.

Mitchell Willet sat on a towel, though you insisted on giving him your chair. With a flashlight, the captain signaled for Río to bring a chair, but Willet asked him to stop.

Clarissa excused herself to go for another walk, and Cora followed her. You lit a cigar, Mother lit a cigarette, and I said, "May I have a glass of wine?"

"No," Mother said.

"Why not?" you said. "Put some hair on his chest."

The captain poured.

"Both of you are abominable," Mother said and looked away.

You picked a loose leaf off your cigar. You said, "Mitchell, what's your yacht? A sixty, seventy footer?"

"Seventy. Want to buy her?"

You laughed. "What am I going to do with a boat that size?"

"I take it you must know Old Kaiser, if you're anchored here," the captain said to Willet.

"We've done a little business together," Willet said.

"It's hard to believe we haven't met," you said to Willet. "It seems your name is always coming up. You weren't at the Chaîne dinner last month, now were you?"

That made him laugh, softly. "I don't like those dinners. Too much wild pheasant and boar for me—"

"I couldn't agree with you more," Mother said.

"But I do think we've met somewhere. . . . I just can't remember," Willet said. "I will say, Missus Lyon, you have a reputation for making all the young men fall for you."

Mother closed her eyes. "I don't see how that's possible. The only young man I know is my son."

"Mitchell just bought Bat Island," the captain said.

"No kidding?" You rose out of your chair and paced the length of the canopy, your wineglass in hand.

"Where's that? Bat Island?" Mother said and then yawned. "Rather ghoulish name, don't you think?"

"It's to the east, below Norman Island, farther east than Buck Island," Willet said. "I have two houses left on it. I may have to tear them down if no one buys them soon. I hate an empty house."

"Darling, Mister Willet may make your dream come true. Why don't we buy a house on this bat-infested Bat Island?" Mother said and gave you a wide smile.

You said, "I assure you the name doesn't do it justice."

"Have you been there, Dad?"

The captain poured more wine while Willet told you that, indeed, the name was appropriate: there were still many bats there and he'd found bat-watching to be a fascinating hobby and why not buy a house.

I thought you should answer me, but you said to Willet, "It's a difficult island to get to. Julia would object to taking a boat or seaplane every time we needed to get away."

"Oh, lovely," Mother said. "Put the blame on me."

The captain wished for music and Willet got to his feet. In his red dinghy, he sped back to his boat. He returned with two short men, both wearing red T-shirts and white pants. One carried a guitar, the other a pair of small bongo drums, and Willet instructed them to stand by the trees and play.

"This is pleasant," Mother said and then Willet offered her British cigarettes.

When no one was looking, I poured myself a little more wine.

"I envy you, Mister Lyon, having two daughters," Willet said. "Do you have another son?"

"No," I said. "I'm going to work for Isla one day." I finished my glass of wine and slid down in the chair.

As if to have a better look at me, Willet tilted up his chin, exposing a hairy neck. Like a chimp.

Clarissa and Cora came back, Clarissa complaining of mosquito bites and Cora saying she wanted to go back to the boat.

Willet said to all of us, "Why not take a tour of my yacht?"

Clarissa and I went with you to Willet's yacht, and Mother and Cora had returned to *Justicia*. Willet's boat was called *So Sara*, after his wife, and its great size prevented it from rocking as much as the captain's boat. The mahogany panels of the cabin were glossy in the glow of the light on deck, and the deck was sprawling and clean, the kind of place where Willet could pace as he thought. I imagined this pale man to have thoughts like these: Shit, Alfonso Menudo and his people are at Saint John. Shit, I should have gone to the Grenadines.

You marched ahead with Willet, neither of you speaking, you several inches taller than Willet, but you didn't walk as fast as he. Clarissa and I lagged behind, pointing out to each other the satin chairs, the silky curtains, the large portholes.

"Look at all the clipper ships," Clarissa said as we entered the main cabin. There was a dining area with etchings of clipper ships on the walls and a lounge area with a television, stereo and bar. Almost everything was white. Mother had once told us, In the old days, if someone wore white, that was a sign of great wealth. The galley was twice as big as my sleeping cabin on *Justicia*. With each new room, I nudged Clarissa and then I said, "It smells like a flower shop in here."

You heard me and said, "What do you have, a load of fresh-cut flowers on board?"

"Something to that effect," Willet said and opened a door next to what he called the master bedroom. Behind the door was a miniature greenhouse, no more than six feet in diameter, with a glass dome, and the stars looked as if they were pasted on the glass. Poppies, daffodils, lilies and green plants I couldn't name grew inside. In the middle of the room, there were large pink roses, and Clarissa stepped inside and inhaled: both Clarissa and Mother loved roses.

Willet told us, "I feel uncomfortable floating on all this water without a bit of land with me."

"Too much for me," you said. "Don't get me wrong, it's certainly beautiful. It's just too much for me."

After we left the greenhouse, Willet opened the master bedroom, where there was a bed and a piano. Clarissa said to Willet, "Do you play?"

"My wife did."

You put your arm around Clarissa. "Clarissa will play. Play the Prelude and Fugue in B major. Isn't that the one I love?"

"I've never played on a boat before," she said. She sat down at the piano and waited for a few seconds and then hurried through a chromatic scale. She stopped to tell me, "The piano's out of tune."

We all sat on the bed.

She went on playing. She played the Bach and then began making something up and I couldn't tell anymore that the piano was out of tune. Willet didn't take his eyes off her and neither did you and then she stopped playing. She blushed, something I'd never seen her do at the piano, and you looked as if someone had stolen something from you. You stood. I wanted to tell her that she shouldn't quit, that she, as you believed, was making a mistake.

Willet said, "Extraordinary, Clarissa. Would you like to top that performance off with a little Louis the Thirteen cognac?"

"Louis the Thirteen? No kidding?" you said.

Willet disappeared into the galley. You told me Clarissa was breaking your heart with her talk about giving up the piano.

When Willet returned, he said to you, "Now I remember where I saw you: on Bat Island. It must have been years ago . . . fifteen years, maybe. You were with a woman at a restaurant. I remember your face. You do have a distinctive face—the deep-set eyes, the square chin. Funny, how this is all coming back to me."

"If it was fifteen years ago, I hope it was Mom you were with," Clarissa said.

You said, "It was more like twenty years ago."

So you had been there.

Willet said, "And now that I think about it—hold on, yes, I'm sure—you had an animal with you at the table. Perhaps the animal had the distinctive face and not you at all." He chuckled. "It was an odd creature . . . what was it?"

"A lemur. It was a gift from the owner of the restaurant. A friend of his had smuggled it in from Madagascar. It was supposed to be a joke." You tapped the bottom of the snifter. "You have a crisp memory."

"A mongoose—yes, it was a mongoose."

"A ring-tailed lemur," you said. "I felt sorry for it; it was very gentle and didn't belong to us. You didn't talk to me, did you?"

"I think my wife did," Willet said. "She probably wanted to take a snapshot of the animal."

"Who were you with, Dad?" I said.

"Could have been one of twenty," you said. "I was a bachelor. I was always going on trips. It's just that you don't forget a lemur."

We got back to *Justicia*, where Mother was smoking a cigarette on the stern. "I was worried," she said. "What took you so long?"

"Oh, we were finding out all about Dad's old girlfriends," Clarissa told her.

"Why don't you kids call it a night?" you said and Clarissa added that the woman Willet had mentioned must have been quite memorable and not the lemur. She then kissed us all and left.

"Has Mitchell Willet a friend on the boat?" Mother said, as I wandered onto the bow, from where I could see Willet's boat, well anchored. I wanted to be living on a boat, I wanted to be older and alone. I snuck toward the stern, didn't let either of you see me, as the canopy hid most of the ladder, and I climbed up the ladder. I almost stepped on Río.

"Shit, scare the hell outa me, man," Río said.

I told him to be quiet, please. In my bare feet, I felt how rough the floor was. "Sorry. I forgot you slept up here."

He told me he hadn't been sleeping, he'd just finished cleaning up after the captain, and that was the most he'd ever said to me.

I said, "Do you live on this boat?"

"No, I live in my own house in Isla Verde, alone. That way people don't order me around. But Menudo's a good boss. He lets me be as free as I want."

Seventeen? Eighteen? Maybe older? He was no doubt free. Without a father, mother or sisters.

Río sneezed, wiped his nose on the back of his wrist, and said, "You oughta sleep. You look tired. Sleep's the next best thing to being with a woman."

"Río, have you ever been to Bat Island?"

I said good night to you and Mother and then went inside the cabin. I collapsed on the couch. The cabin was furnished in blue and red. The captain kept a pile of magazines on the coffee table, *Fortune, Travel & Leisure* and a *Fashion*, which had a bold headline that read: "How to Improve Sex, with Respect." I thought of sex and couldn't imagine the two of you ever being so close, doing what I'd seen in the magazines my friends always showed me. I didn't have to buy those magazines; you already had them. I could imagine me with Teresa—the way she shook her hips that time in class so only I could see. The way I took an old piece of Mother's velvet and wet it. Velvet softer than my hands.

I put my ear close to the curtain over the open porthole and heard you say: "Cora, she's marked. I worry."

I couldn't guess what you were talking about, as Mother said angrily, "You make her sound like a branded cow."

You again, after some silence: "I heard Fiona flew in from Rome last week."

"Russell's getting rotten press on that Fiona." I knew Fiona and Russell were new friends of yours, but I'd never met them.

"Fiona's a devout Catholic," you said.

"And so?" Mother said. "He's a Reformed Jew. What's the difference? If they marry, one will give in to the other's faith. It's always the way. . . . Alfonso says Mitchell Willet has a bidet on the yacht. Is that true, David?"

You were laughing and then you said, "You used to like that."

"Yes." Mother's voice was soft. I parted the curtain on the porthole and saw that you were standing.

"Julia, what is it? Every time I touch you, you—"

"Every time you touch me, it's for you, not me. Please, we're on someone's boat."

She said good night and I met her at the door. She patted my head, murmuring how sorry she was that I couldn't sleep, and she strolled into her cabin.

"Why aren't you in bed?" you said to me.

"I was in the cabin." I heard it all, I wanted to say, so you could tell me why Mother didn't want you to hold her. "What happened to the lemur, Dad?"

"Oh, the ring-tailed lemur. Willet's a strange one, bringing up things like that, making them sound so mysterious." I thought you sounded drunk. "He talks up a ball of wax, a bunch of bananas—"

I said, "You don't like him."

"I like everyone, Michael."

"The class is called *Arachnida*. And there are two families. *Buthidae* and *chactidae*. Wait, let me see the difference between the two." It was the next morning and Cora was reading to me from the captain's book. The sunlight, though weak at that hour, made her blond hair appear whiter. "I don't know. They don't explain the difference right here. Oh, guess how many eyes a scorpion has?"

"One."

"Six to twelve, depending on the class. Shows how little you know. . . . Listen to this: After scorpions have sex, the female sometimes eats the male."

"Then she eats her children?" I said.

Clarissa and Mother came out of the cabin, which smelled of ham. Río was cooking breakfast.

Mother said to Cora, "Why don't you brush your hair?" When you walked out, she said to you, "Well, don't you look spiffy in your tan. Doesn't your dad look grand?"

The captain climbed down the ladder from the tower, and I wondered whether he was thinking: *This family—what a family: so wonderful. And what a father. Steady, no blowing that man down.*

"Shall we invite Mitchell over for breakfast?" the captain said.

"Come on, *Capitán,*" you said, "give our stomachs a rest. Let's shove off."

"I'll feed your tribe, if you don't mind. Río," the captain called, "keep it simple: shirred eggs and no salmon."

"Salmon?" Mother said.

"You like that, sweet Julia?" the captain said.

"If David's not feeling hungry, he doesn't have to eat," Mother said. "If he's not feeling sociable, Alfonso, it's best we don't invite that Mitchell over. After all, who will talk to him?"

"Sweet Julia; as always, you have a point." The captain smiled and bellowed again: "Río, *el salmón.*"

Then you told us you'd made a decision. You wanted to buy a house on Bat Island; Bat Island was beautiful and it was definitely worth the trouble to get there. Mother was about to say something, but you held up your hand to silence her and then kissed the top of her head. She blushed.

You turned to the captain and patted his shoulder. "Alfonso, what do you think?"

He thought it was the perfect end to the trip.

Overflow

ather cleverly explained to Clarissa, Michael and me that the news was due to an intriguing proposition he and Aunt Nadia had come up with. But I suspected that the "news" had been simmering in his head for some time. First, he'd bought a stone cottage on Bat Island (we all saw Polaroids). Then, he bought a duplex apartment in Manhattan. We were moving to New York in May 1972, the twenty-eighth, to be precise. Clarissa dreamed of shopping for all four seasons. She flitted around the house wearing a new cashmere scarf she'd ordered from a catalogue. Michael wanted to go to plays; about to turn twelve, suddenly he had drama on his mind. As for me, I felt like an old woman dependent on a cane she accidentally loses down a street grating. I didn't want to leave the island. The idea of a city, of millions of people rushing to subways, appalled me. In New York, I imagined, everything would be considerably worse than in Puerto Rico; even the sewers would be dirtier. I began admiring the sewers around my house, looking for unusual treasures in them. Mother soon sat me down: "Clarissa said you've begun to, well, dear, sewer-watch, I think she said. Your sister says you've been sitting on the curb staring into the sewer. But, dear, there are rats with rabies in the sewer. And . . . and bats, too."

"You mean alligators."

"Cora," she said, "I forbid you to hang around those filthy sewers. Cora, are you listening!"

But I enjoyed Mother's wondering why I spent my time on a curb. Strangers stopped and asked me if I'd lost my way or if I'd dropped something down the sewer. I told them I was preparing myself for the detestable aspects of New York. I'd been to New York on vacation several times. I recognized how aptly our unexpected move there reflected my lack of control over my future.

Early one morning, around two, I woke up perspiring and felt a sensation not too unlike a snake traveling through my stomach. It was raining, the windows were coated with water, and I bled into the toilet. I'd clearly broken something inside. This was nothing like the period I'd just begun to have a few months before. This was another overflow of blood, as if I'd ruptured my stomach. I was repulsed, chilled; yes, me: the once-equatorial Cora.

I went to Clarissa. She was asleep on her stomach. I shook her and whispered somewhat furiously, "Don't tell anyone."

"What?" she whined. "What's wrong?"

"Swear not to tell anyone."

She crossed her heart; I told.

"Come in here," she said. She opened her bed to me. "Don't worry. I think that happens sometimes. Just don't worry, okay?"

I closed my eyes. Soon enough I was back in the bathroom. Clarissa, I hoped, didn't hear me leave. But when I returned to her bed she'd set up a game of checkers and told me we should play until I got tired. A magnificent idea—a ploy to take my thoughts off my body. Yet during the game she plagued me with questions. Did anything hurt? Could I sleep? How many times had it happened? I told her it didn't really hurt. I paid little attention to the game. I told myself, This hurts a lot.

The next afternoon, Mother, wheedling her way into my bedroom, said, "Clarissa says you're bleeding. You must tell Mummy all about this."

I thought: How shall I describe this? In a British fashion? *Oh, bloody shit!* No doubt I should be polite, as Mother would like me to be: I should use euphemisms and, if only I knew them, medical terms. "Clarissa was dreaming," I said, though I wanted to say I was the one dreaming.

"You're fibbing and I don't appreciate it," Mother said and then left, muttering how I was only punishing myself. I searched the house for Clarissa, but she had, Mother reported, gone to visit a friend.

For comfort, I gravitated, feeling sluggish, to a sewer. There was an extremely appealing one at the end of our block. I sat at the curb and stared at the black water from the gutters as it slipped through the grating. I spotted what looked like a pink plastic shower curtain ring in the gutter; I caught it. I forced it on my wrist and then couldn't get it off. Through the grating, I thought I saw a plump rat sneering up at me. I tried to poke my hand through the iron bars, but my hand was too large. Two dead goldfish streamed into my view. Large and big-eyed, they got stuck and lay like leaves. Sea horses followed, that color green like old copper. Nothing looked dirty down there. Behind the sea horses came a pink and white rattle, an open box of lozenges, a syringe, several uprooted flowers and a tiny doll with wet red hair. I wished I could save the sea horses, at least; the fish were surely dead.

A young woman who appeared to have just come from the beach—her toes were sandy—stopped by me. She wore round green sunglasses. She said, "What ya got there?" She sat next to me, her damp hair touching my shoulder. She smelled like artificial coconut. Out of her beach bag she took a bunch of tiny sandy shells and began dropping them down the grating. "There, that's better. There's something to look at."

"Who are you?" I said.

"Tina. I go with Jack Hall. Do you know him? He lives there, but he's not home now. I'm waiting for him."

"I'm waiting to get better," I said.

"You're sick?"

"I'm not telling anyone until it goes away," I said. Here, I thought, was a perfect example of the peace on the island, this sandy woman taking time to chat as the sun turned the sky purple and orange.

"Take some," she said and handed me a few shells; one had a hermit crab in it. As I put the crab on the sidewalk, I noticed that the woman's right hand was blistered.

She said, "I have a feeling I'll be waiting for a while. Where is that guy?"

Within minutes, a blue convertible Chevrolet pulled in at Jack's house. Jack was with a woman. She rested her blond head on his shoulder. They were laughing and laughing; the radio was blasting salsa. They didn't see us.

Tina said, punching her beach bag, "Now *I* feel sick."

I felt sorry for this Tina. And so I left her right away. I hadn't energy to feel sorry for anyone but myself. I thought: No more charms in that sewer.

At home, I walked toward the pool. I sat on the bench under the *flamboyán* tree and fell into a heavy sleep. When I awoke, Father was standing over me, prepared, I could tell, to siphon the truth from me. "Your sister's never lied before. She says you're sick and I believe her," he began as he wrapped his golf sweater around me.

When Clarissa got home, I banned her from my room. She spent the evening with Mother on the terrace, sipping iced tea. I was content: left alone, I'd figure out a cure. But in no time, Father and Mother were creeping into my room. They seemed so united, I was momentarily grateful I'd begun to bleed.

Father said, touching the pink band on my wrist, "Tell us what's wrong."

Mother said, rubbing her hands, "Yes, no more fibs."

"Do I look sick?" I knew I didn't. My cheeks were unusually rosy. My eyes seemed brightened by an emergency light within me.

But the next day I woke up unable to move. A dizziness swept over me. In the middle of the night, a tremendous amount of blood had seeped out of me, and having carefully checked for lesions or wounds and finding none, I quivered in bed and resigned myself to telling. Fearful, uncertain and exhausted that morning, a particularly humid morning which made my bare soles stick to the kitchen tiles, I told Mother about my body's secret. I tried to get the pink band off my wrist. No luck.

Mother immediately phoned a New York doctor. As she explained my symptoms, she began to cry. My stomach hurt; the jabbing came without warning. I couldn't tell—and I panicked over this: was this only fear twisting inside my guts, or was this my stomach bleeding? I looked at Mother's white hands, such graceful hands, reaching for a tissue. I listened to her diminishing sobs as she got off the phone. She picked up a red rag lying on an empty cupboard shelf, where she used to keep a colorful set of cookie jars, the kind that fit into one another. With the rag, she dabbed under her eyes.

Those jars reminded me of a Russian doll Clarissa had. The doll opened like an egg to reveal inside a smaller doll, and inside that, an even smaller one. There were five in all. But the fifth one, the smallest, contained hundreds of ivory-shaped dolls the size of ants. As Mother made herself some tea, I kept thinking of the minuscule ivory pieces. To get to them, a child liked to open one doll after another. I'd do the opposite, I thought. I'd always begin with the tiny dolls. I'd pour them into the smallest doll, then fit the small into the larger doll until the largest stood alone, intact, containing everything.

Mother said, "Very well. We'll pack tonight and catch a morning plane. We'll get you to a reliable doctor in New York. But not to worry, this isn't serious; it can't possibly be."

I pictured an assembly of doctors, all chattering and playfully pulling me apart. I could already hear their rising voices: *Here's another little one, crumbling into pieces.*

Taking Mother's hand, I said, "You'll get me better."

Rincón

The waves slapped against the beach. I thought about Cora's bleeding. Tad said to me, "That Tickle kid . . . Clarissa, he just vanished."

"I'd rather not think about him," I said. Instead, I thought of the doctor in New York. He said Cora had ulcerative colitis; it was acute. No one in the family had ever been seriously sick before.

"Let's sing. Let's sing our national anthem," María said. She began to sing. Her voice was deep and soft. She braided her thick hair. Tad, Julio and I started to sing, too. Julio swept María to her feet. They danced in the sand. Tad tossed a cigarette in the air and caught it in his mouth.

"Look at the formations," I said. I pointed to the moonlit waves.

Tad's flashlight followed my hand. "What are you looking at?"

"Can't you see?"

María said, "The fire's going out. You're not very good at keeping it going, Tad."

"*Necesítas un hombre,*" Julio said. He threw sticks onto the fire. Julio and María had been sleeping together for two years. María had black eyes, a wide-bridged nose and a gap between her teeth. Julio was small. He had quick eyes.

"What are you looking at?" Tad said again.

I said, "I feel guilty."

"You *are* guilty." Tad slung his arm around me. He smelled like cigarettes. "But let's give her a fair trial."

Julio and María both squatted and stared at me.

"You've disobeyed your father," Julio said. "An unforgivable sin. We need a jury."

"I say hang her," María said and giggled. Her long hair almost caught fire. But Julio lifted her braid toward his mouth. "We'll use this as rope," he said.

My father had forbidden me to go camping at Rincón. There'd been several bomb scares in his supermarkets. Then a bomb had gone off in one. Then Richard Tickle was kidnapped. His father received two notes. My father told me terrorists had sent a list to the FBI. Our name was on the list. Suddenly FALN, CAL and Independentistas were household words.

I was seventeen and a virgin. I wanted to sleep with Tad at a beach. The bad politics meant nothing to me. I wanted to leave the east island and my father miles behind. I told my father I was sleeping at María's. I lied to ease his worry. My favorite lies are those that help soothe other people.

"Let's walk." The sun was setting. The sky looked orange.

"Aren't you dying to go to bed?" Tad whispered.

"No, I want to walk. I won't be able to walk around like this for a long time. New York won't have any sand, trees or water."

He poured light onto the sand before us. He shut off the light. Our camp was on a plot of grass near a surfers' snack shop. We were on the beach now. The waves were rough.

"I wonder what'll change when I leave?" I said.

"You're leaving soon," he said. "What feels different?"

"Cora's sick."

We walked to a tree stump where the beach ended. We sat on the stump, facing a narrow road that had one streetlamp. Tad smoked another cigarette. With the butt he traced the appendix scar along his stomach. After the operation, he'd begun to stutter. Now he liked to speak in fragments. He seemed blue to me that evening. His eyes were the color of the ocean. His black hair looked navy.

From the south a horse came, breathing hard. Two young boys were riding it. They were hitting the horse with a stick. They couldn't see us, it seemed. Tad motioned for me to be quiet.

The boy riding in front said the horse was good for nothing. He said he'd paid twenty dollars for it. The boy in back was small. He patted the other boy on the shoulder. The smaller boy jumped off and said, *"Carne al carbón."* The taller boy slipped off. They beat the horse more.

"Stop them," I said.

Tad put his hand over my mouth.

The horse whinnied and tried to run away. The larger boy held on to its reins. The horse made a weak attempt at bucking and then thudded to the ground.

I pushed Tad's hand away. "Stop them, Tad. I'll stop them." They were still thrashing the horse. Then they shot it. I hadn't thought they had a gun. I stood. Tad began kissing me hard and I began crying. We heard a second gunshot and, soon after, running.

"It hurt a little," I told Tad as he rested on top of me. We were in our tent. It was six in the morning.

"I guess it would."

I said, "We should have stopped them."

"I figured they had a gun. You think they'd give a second thought to riddling us with holes in the middle of nowhere? You think their catchable. They ain't." He held me. "It was real good, right?"

"I hate it here."

"But look," he said and opened the tent. The sun burned

through the morning clouds. The ocean was as rough as it had been the night before. We heard María singing. Julio was striking matches.

"After what happened last night," I said, "I'm happy to be leaving."

"Hey, you're leaving me, too. Don't be so happy. And *two* things happened last night." He hugged me, kissed me.

"I'm not coming back."

Julio made a fire and then coffee. I took two records from my knapsack and went by the fire. I'd bought María and Julio Bach's *Die Kunst der Fuge:* The Art of Fugue.

I used to play fugues to warm up. My father had bought me *Die Kunst der Fuge* after I stopped my piano lessons. He said Jesús, a conductor of the Puerto Rico Symphony, had recommended the piece. Jesús had said the fugues were "amazing." He gave my father the score. I found the sheets of music in the wrapping of the album cover. I studied every note.

Bach was going blind when he composed the fugues. He wrote eighteen and died before finishing the last. Each one is based on a D-minor theme of twelve notes. I've always liked minor keys.

In the final fugue, Bach uses notes in the countersubject that, in German notation, represent B, A, C, H. B flat is B; B natural is H. For the whole *cantus firmus* he uses notes that represent J., S., B, A, C, H. His inversions and his chromatic figures pleased me. So did his canons. But the inclusion of his name amazed me.

I didn't tell my father how much I admired the record. I just thanked him for it. I thought he'd equate my liking the piece with a desire to continue to play the piano.

I never had to tell my mother how I felt about the piano. She sensed my attitudes. Once, when I was twelve, I combined a minor diatonic scale with a major one. My mother was behind me, watching. I stopped playing. She said, "What was that little song?" And I said, "Scales, Mom." She said, "Aren't you modest? I could tell by the way you were moving your shoulders that that was one of your little songs." Several years later, she overheard me practicing the scales again. I'd become much better. Yet she said, "Those scales aren't much fun for you. Are they tiresome, darling?"

What if I'd stayed with the piano? I was certain my skill would become mechanical. My composition would become imitative. My confidence would become arrogance. I'd be stunted. That was almost as painful to me as becoming blind.

María said, "We're supposed to give you a gift. You're the one who's leaving."

"Why do I feel as if you guys are leaving me?"

She smiled. Her family had just moved to Santurce. They used to live in Bayamón. Her father had been a supervisor in a sugarcane factory before it became automated. He'd then been hired as manager of a bank in Isla Verde. She said that ever since he'd moved, he was too tired to sleep at night. He was too tired to finish his sentences. I knew María would appreciate the unfinished *Die Kunst der Fuge.*

I gave Tad Chopin's nocturnes. He said, "Chopin," pronouncing the name like "chop." He kissed the record.

Julio stood and struck a coconut against a large rock. He broke the coconut open. He took out a jackknife and cut pieces of meat for everyone. As I ate, Tad picked me up. He tossed me into the ocean.

"Dios mío," María said. We drove off the road to avoid the horse. It was now eight in the morning. The horse's legs were limp and to its side. Its snout was rusted with blood. A dirty blanket and tattered reins were twisted about its head and body. María said once more, *"Dios mío."*

"That's the first dead horse I've ever seen," Tad said.

Julio said he'd seen a dead pony when he was a boy.

I felt the absence that came with thinking that I might never be with these friends again.

We passed a family who were barbecuing a pig and a few chickens on the side of the road. The meat was suspended on a stick between two tree trunks. There were hot coals in the sand. The woman poked the pig with a knife. The man and the boy sat on the ground, eating some chicken. They tossed the bones into the road.

Part Two

Clocks

O
n my knees, I fingered the carpet and studied the cuckoo clock above your new reading chair. At noon, a wooden bird came out, bony and blue, with a sharp beak, which, when open, said nothing. The clocks were the start of your collection and Mother had already hung four on the den wall. Each one allowed time to pass in a purr and never with a tick. The two clocks above the desk were both early nineteenth century, with gold etchings, but they didn't work; one clock was fixed on noon and the other on three. Between the door and the bar stood a grandfather clock made of mahogany. The room looked and felt as if it belonged to you, Father: neat, gracious.

It was mid-September 1972. We'd moved into a large two-floor apartment on Beekman Place, with a view of the East River; Clarissa was at school in Middlebury; and you were in Saint Croix, checking on your stores after some terrorists had shot several American tourists at the Fountain Valley Golf Club there. The guests had been robbed, too, and no one was sure, you phoned to tell me, which terrorist group was responsible. I walked out of the den and to the small elevator. When we'd first moved in, Cora and I had taken the elevator, the two of us wondering: what could we use this narrow thing for?

In the living room, heavy streams of sunlight flooded the fireplace and hit the Chinese urns in each corner. A baby grand was supposed to come in a few weeks for whenever, I guessed, Clarissa came home from school, and there was a space left for it. I didn't like the living room. Mother did, yet she refused to sit on the white couch and chairs, choosing instead to smoke in a sturdy wooden rocker in front of the fireplace, flicking her cigarette against an ashtray on her lap.

Now she lay stomach down under the living room coffee table, insisting she'd seen a bug, brought in, no doubt, she said, from the plant store deliverymen. I said, "The cuckoo clock is broken." She waved me off with a sweep of her hand. "The cuckoo? I had the shop owner take out its voice. Who needs a bird that sings every hour?" She whistled, imitating the sound of a cuckoo. "I despise birds anyway, Michael. And your father knows it all too well. But he loved the thing, so I bought it for him." She held her neck with one hand and said, "That spider's gotten away."

I said, "What good is a cuckoo clock if it doesn't sing?"

She grunted, her dismissal, so I left the room and quickly spotted the spider. I returned to the clocks.

School was in a ten-story building with an enclosed rooftop gym that had balancing beams, movable basketball hoops and shiny oak bleachers. When we played basketball, captains wanted me on their teams, but during breaks or in the locker room, while everyone criticized this guy's point or that guy's miss, I was quiet. And regardless of Cora telling me how cute I was, how Gina, her new girlfriend, thought I was "to die for," I felt like a stick that someone could toss away.

By early October, I wore two sweaters, two of everything, but still felt cold, so instead of walking to the bus stop I ended up getting into cabs with Cora. Mother forbade Cora, who'd been sick the past few months, to ride the subways or buses. A block or two before school, Cora would say to the cabdriver, Excuse me, sir, would you let me off here?

One morning, we got out of the cab and Penn, a guy in my math class, came up behind me and tapped me on my shoulder, saying, "Hey, guy, how's it going?" He wore a white baseball cap stained with black spots, like a Dalmatian's skin. He had blond hair and brown eyes, and his smile was slanted a little.

I introduced him to Cora and he shook her hand, then what'd he do: kiss her glove. Cora giggled and dashed ahead, and Penn said, "How come you don't talk to anyone? It's good for you, y'know? Your sister's cute."

Cute. What did he know? Cora was pale, sick. Skinny. Face like a blowfish. Poisoned from steroids. And you'd soothe her: But, baby, it gives you some flesh, makes you look healthy. That time, she ran into her room: studying herself in the mirror. Where's Cora? Not in that mirror. Opening her eyes wide with her fingers, pulling back her lips. Examining her teeth as if she were a horse. Or a slave for sale. "Did I tell you, Michael? The doc says my teeth can break easily now, from the pills." Drying wishbones. Short end.

"So what do you think?" Penn said and stopped in front of school.

"About what?" We passed through the gate.

"Do you want to smoke a joint after school?"

"I don't really smoke," Penn said. "But I could get pot if you wanted." He puffed on a cigarette and offered me one, which I took. We were blocks away from our school, outside a boarded-up media school, the letters of its sign cracking, and after I lit the cigarette, I tossed it into the gutter.

"What a waste, man. You didn't have to take it," Penn said. "You surf?"

"No."

"I'd be a great surfer, but I need a real ocean, like a hot ocean, y'know?" He rubbed his hands against his pants and cursed himself for having lost his gloves. "Like I've been to Vermont, to Massachusetts and all those New Englandy kind of places, and every summer I go to this lakey camp called Minotikawa and I swim in the lake, sail in the lake, until I feel like my spit tastes like lake." He dragged on his cigarette. "I don't have a sister, I don't have a brother, and my father died five years ago, and so, ergo, no dad. But that's cool with me. Mom's a hotshot. Every day she goes out in her Giorgio Armani suits. She's big over at Paine Webber. And she has a guy. And that's cool for her. Don't think she's no fun and all work. His name is William Pinsky. Yeah, that's his name." He flicked his cigarette into some bushes. "So anyway, you want to go to the Plaza? They have a great roof. I know all about a good roof."

He gave me instructions: "When we go inside, we just stroll through the lobby like we belong, our noses high up like we're balancing balls on them. Then we go straight for the telephones; that's where the elevators are."

On the top floor there was a door that said ROOF. The corridor smelled like the gasoline at airports. Penn said we shouldn't stay in the staircase, so we opened the door and I thought of an alarm. He said workmen had been repairing the roof for the past few months and one workman had told him the alarm was disconnected. "The guests don't know that," Penn said. He grinned.

The roof was windy. I looked at the park, the horses hooked to the carriages, the stone walls and the moving cars, and the smoke streaming out of the buses. I saw some boys wearing black yarmulkes, skittering behind a fat woman, one boy taking his yarmulke off and behind them two German shepherds flanked a man in black. I kicked loose asphalt, while Penn complained that his fingers were getting cold. I said, "How'd your dad die?"

He hit the wall with a flat hand and said, "I can't believe you fucking asked that; no one asks me that. He had a heart attack. I was nine. I had this friend, Jake; he never asked about my dad and he knew him. Anyway, Jake moved to Colorado." He walked over to a pile of green plastic bags covered with dirt and from

under one took out a Jim Beam bottle. "Mike, look, workman's compensation. A construction guy told me that. Have a shot."
"Don't call me Mike. I don't like it."
"Got a middle name?"
"Justin."
"Okay, I'll call you Just."
I took the bottle and drank. He took two sips, handed it to me, then our drinking was over, and he tucked the bottle back into its plastic bag.

Penn said, "When I was like five or six, my dad used to take me to our roof and have me throw over a penny and make a wish. So go ahead, give it a try."
"I should go home."
Rain fell on us and I started for the door, but he said, "Shit, Michael, it's bad luck to leave without making the wish."
I fished out a penny, threw it over the side into an alley and wished for a snowstorm that'd shut down the city. Penn folded a dollar bill like a paper airplane, and as he let the dollar float down to the alley, he said, "A bum'll have a hot pretzel on me. Your wish won't even feed a bird."

"This is great. I've never had dinner like this before," Penn said and gnawed on the bone. Cora, Penn and I were in the den, stack tables in front of us, the television on *Star Trek*, each of us facing a slab of meat with a bone, potatoes and string beans. After we'd left the roof, I'd declined his invitation to eat dinner at his house, then I invited him to eat at mine. Mother was upstairs in the bath (had been, Cora said, for over an hour). I picked my glass up, thinking we must look like robots, eating, watching, drinking, and suddenly a robot appeared on the screen.

Then you came home, met Penn, and told us about an accident on First Avenue that had cost you an extra five dollars in the cab. You headed for the bookcase and took out a book on wine. "Here it is: *chantepleure, chantepleure*. Someone asked me what the spigot was called in French. I thought it was *cantas*-something. It's been bothering me all day."

I knew that. The spigot. Hadn't you told me: a spigot hisses—

no, a spigot sings when opened? Wine spilling out. Weeping out
of the barrel. Who wanted to know? "Who wanted to know?"
"The wine buyer. A funny man, the new wine buyer." You
loosened your tie.

"*Chantefleure,*" Cora said. "I like that."

"*Chantepleure,*" you said to Cora and ruffled her hair. Then
you said to me, "How's school? I hope you're making yourself
known, as your father always does."

Penn said, "He is, sir, he really is."

I said nothing. It was eight o'clock and the doors of the cuckoo
clock were about to open. When they did, you laughed once,
twice, and then said, "Penn, would you believe this: my wife
gives me a cuckoo clock that doesn't say Cuckoo. See, the bird
only pivots on the first tone. That's unusual." You put your knee
on the ottoman and stared at the bird until it shut itself in the
clock again.

It was an early Sunday morning and the sun blistered through
November clouds, warming the roof of the Plaza. Penn and I had
made our slipping onto the roof a routine, this being our seventh
time. Once Penn had given a ten-dollar bill and a pack of cigarettes to a porter who threatened to find out which room we
were in; for the next week I shared my allowance with Penn. I
wrapped my coat tightly around me and pulled in my knees. I
said to Penn, "What did your father do?"

"He was an architect. A really good one. He designed lots of
things, even churches."

"Do you go to church?"

He said, "I don't believe in religion. I don't need it."

"I'm not going to have a bar mitzvah. My mother said I
shouldn't if I didn't feel right about it."

"Your mom's boss."

I thought: No, my mother's Catholic and switches to Judaism
from time to time. What did that feel like, I wondered, having
no faith to fear, having only the constant back-and-forth? I
looked at a pigeon pecking at gravel in a corner of the roof.
"When I told my dad I didn't want to have one, he didn't yell at

me. He said, 'I'm just disappointed.' " I threw a crumb of cement at the bird and missed. "Maybe I'd do it now."

"Come on then, we'll bar mitzvah you here," Penn said and hit the garbage bags with his mitt.

I said, angry suddenly, "He should've taken me to the temple, he should've made me have a bar mitzvah."

Penn took a cigarette out, put it in his mouth, and said, "You're too serious, y'know?"

"Give me a penny. All I have is a dollar." A nickel landed near my feet and I picked it up and tossed it hard over the side of the roof.

Lighting a match, Penn said, "How come you have to talk about your father so much?"

Soon we were crossing the street to Central Park and walking toward the reservoir. Penn handed me his mitt, ran into a Frisbee game, caught the disk and sent it flying to a young boy across the field. The boy sent the Frisbee back to Penn, who snapped it up, threw it to the other boy and in the same motion turned to me and said he didn't feel like going to the reservoir. "I'm going to leave this city soon."

I said, "And do what?"

"Get a boat. What are you going to do?"

"Act."

"Why do that for a living? I act just about every day. With just about everyone. There are three main ways to do it, noble Just. And it all comes down to getting into someone else's rhythm. One: Stay quiet and listen to the person. Two: Ask a lot of questions so you can go with the current of their thinking. And three: Agree with part of what they say, 'cause if you agree with it all, they'll be onto you. There's your lesson. But go ahead: become an actor anyway." He put his hands over his heart and said, "Oh, Juliet."

For as short a time as I knew him, I'd never seen him get angry or upset for long, and now I felt that his apparent happiness was probably a form of acting. Maybe his mother didn't really know him, and I would never come to know him either. To me, he looked characterless as his hands motioned to an invisible Juliet on a balcony, and I imagined the true Penn—a beast—writhing inside his body, hurting his chest as it clawed to come out. I swore to myself that I'd watch for signs: a moment when Penn would forget his guise and appear wounded.

He waved to a classmate of ours who approached with heavy steps, wearing a jacket and a football jersey ripped at the waist. His name was Peter Wescott and I'd never talked to him. He ran up to us, his chubby hand carrying a football, and he said, "Hey, Penn, nice day. What are you guys up to?" He had a thick New York accent.

"Play ball, walk, then do somethin' else," Penn said, without looking at Peter.

Peter buttoned his jacket, hugged the football and stood with his big feet spread apart. He was in my history class, a loud guy, always had his eye on Rachel Wise, a blonde.

He said, "Hey, don't go through the tunnel. Some spicks are there, throwing rocks. Bad news. They almost hit this buddy of mine, Jason. Know Jason Eaton? Anyway, ya better not go that way. They—" He stopped and looked at me. "Hey, wait—Mike here speaks their language. So, Penn, maybe you're cool, after all: you've got your own spick beside you for protection." He slapped Penn on the arm.

"Don't be a Wesnott," Penn said.

"Touchy. I see Rico boy is teaching you a word or two."

I crossed my eyes slightly, made him a blur. No word for him. The word for beyond nothing? I thought if I were an actor, I'd terrify him: I'd yell, I'd hit, I'd make myself known. I brought him into focus. Mother getting in my head, saying: *And don't, for God's sake, tell everyone you're from Puerto Rico. It's not that it's something to be ashamed of. . . . I'm only telling you for your own good.*

Peter spread his feet wide apart and told me, "Speak some Spanish for me. Tell me how I can tell those asshole Ricans to fuck off."

"Fuck off," I said.

Peter spit at my feet.

Still looking at him, I wiped one shoe with the sole of the other.

He said, "I wouldn't fight you; you probably have a switch-blade."

I hit him in the jaw, the first time I'd ever hit to hurt someone. I hit him again and then hit him a third time and then again, and Penn started pulling me away. He told Peter that his tooth was bleeding, and Peter held his hand over his mouth; he started crying. Penn and I walked off through the Frisbee game, toward the tunnel, both of us running now, my face hot. When we came to the reservoir, Penn said, "You should've stopped hitting him."

The following Sunday, after Penn and I played baseball in the park, I crossed the bridge, heading home alone. I liked walking alone, pretending to be different men who passed me by: an old man who mumbled to himself, a sanitation man who stabbed at papers in the grass, a man on a bike carrying a baby on his back. And I thought Penn's way of acting wasn't true, because he'd always stay inside himself and simply put on a new mood with a lie or a story. I walked through the Sheep Meadow, thinking I'd leave the park on Central Park South. I saw an old woman wearing a red apron. A bandanna was knotted around her black hair and she swept behind trees with a tattered broom, brushing dirt from bush to bush. Homeless yet tending her home, she didn't hear or watch me pass by. Someone had spilled a bag of M&M's along the path and I crushed several with one or two steps. It was less crowded once I left the meadow and drifted up to the carousel. The ride was stopped and I watched a little girl who pushed aside other children to get to a yellow horse in the second row. She had trouble mounting the horse.

Then I noticed you several feet away. Your suede jacket looked too big and your shoulders were hunched up as your elbows balanced on the rail, your hands meeting in a fist. I didn't walk up to you right then but just watched you turn your gaze from the child on the mustard horse to a terrier cracking its leash and snapping at pigeons that were eating peanuts on the ground. Then I said, "Dad, what are you doing here?"

"Well, look at this! I'm walking, just walking." You zipped your jacket, fiddled with the cuff so it covered your watch. "What are you doing all alone?"

"I just left Penn."

You nodded and pointed to the carousel. "Remember when I used to take you here? Clarissa would remember. Every New Year's, you used to get on the same horse with Clarissa. That black one there. You'd wait for that horse even if it meant missing a ride."

I looked at the painted horse with its menacing open mouth and square teeth, its gold mane and tail, its saddle decorated with a snarling leopard head. Behind the black horse, a white horse with an unkempt blue mane and half-closed black eyes glided up and down. I said, "I think Clarissa used to call that one Her Majesty." The carousel started up, making the clown faces in the inner post pulse in and out every time the drum sounded. I remembered once being frightened by one of the faces—the fat-lipped clown with a wide sneer and a beige tongue.

"Let's go," you said.

"What'd you do all morning?" I asked.

"Dusted off my wine bottles. You wonder where all that dust comes from. Want to stop by my office on the way home?"

"That'd be good."

We started walking toward the skating rink and passed a teenage girl with buckteeth who stood complaining about a dead pigeon at the foot of the water fountain; she wanted a drink of water. I almost stopped to kick the pigeon out of the way, but you were walking fast and I didn't want you to get ahead of me.

"Get that light, would you?" you said after opening the door that had ISLA printed on it. Beyond a receptionist's desk, a hall held several offices with windows overlooking Park Avenue. We entered the third office, which was large and painted cream, and right away you picked up an envelope on the desk. You tucked the envelope under your arm and said, "This Fountain Valley massacre has done a number on our business in Saint Croix. There can't be any redemption for terrorists. What kind of intelligence plans such pointed tragedies?"

Staring at a painting of a fleet of ships, some with broken masts, some intact, all ships floating on air, I thought: Terrorists do damage to get what they want. And I thought: You do damage by going away; by going away, somehow you get what you want. Maybe one day I'd do damage to get what I want. . . . "I like the painting," I said.

"Aunt Nadia found that. I call it 'Icarus of the Marines.' I forget what it's really called."

The painting showed several tiny ships that looked almost like sea gulls. And a man overboard. The piece took up the whole wall. The opposite wall had six windows, the kind that didn't open. We were on the thirty-third floor. A box of Cuban cigars sat on the desk and the smell of their smoke was still in the room. I saw that the wastebasket was full. I said, "Were you here already?"

"I stopped by on my way to the park, to finish off some work. What do you think of the place?"

I leaned against a window, picturing your office in Hato Rey, the low building connected to the long warehouse, the palms lining the parking lot and so many more people. And Icarus, Icarus, which one was Icarus? He flew? I said, "There's not much room."

"Yes, well . . . who knew it'd be so cramped here? And who knew I'd be going back to Puerto Rico so much? I need to be here for the new stores and there for the old." You handed me a pen with *Isla* printed on it. "You miss home."

Pushing myself off the window, I thought I should surprise you by saying, as Penn probably would, that I loved New York and the apartment and the school. My arm ached from having thrown the ball too hard and I said, yawning a little, "I'm fine."

"Tired? Tired's counterproductive, Michael. A state of mind. I never get tired."

Look at you: zipped-up insomniac. Shut off the light. Slow twist of a key.

Photos

In her white hands Mother cupped a bowl of steaming porridge, its cinnamon smell growing stronger as she heedfully stepped toward the bed. I resented staying in my pretty little bed. But I thought: Better this bed than a strange one, and I told her, "You're so right, Mom. Who needs a hospital?"

"Your own room is the safest place to be," she said and then handed me a small cup marked *Cora's pills,* which contained two cortisone pills and one white pill for stomach spasms. Sometimes she offered me a sleeping pill. Why not? At thirteen, I wasn't ashamed of my weaknesses; I didn't want to be brave. I'd take one when my humiliation became sharper than my stomach pain.

Having been in remission seven months, I was sick again in April, and now, in May, I felt like a sewer rat with rabies, or something close to it. I'd gone to three doctors; the second had diagnosed my illness, and the third, Dr. Wole, had said I should see a psychiatrist, ". . . the general belief being that such intestinal disorders are psychosomatic."

Balancing the bowl on my belly, Mother cooed and said, "I'm going to become a *curandero*." She mispronounced the Spanish. "I've just been reading about one. He's from this tribe . . . oh, perhaps not . . . no," she mumbled and looked past me to the windows. "Anyway, he lives in this village called *El Triunfo*. And he heals the sick with all sorts of lovely things: leaves, potions, sticks and nectars." She snapped her fingers, red nails glistening. "Damn, I forgot to get the pear nectar. . . ."

"Go on about the healer."

She went on. I imagined the boy wincing, poison swimming in his bloodstream after the bite of the *Barba amarilla*. The healer fed him a paste of butterfly leaf, cedron, snakeroot and black tobacco, then sucked the poison out of the bite and patched it with sap. Mother hesitated: was the plant *Candela flandis* or *Camela flemish?*

I was astonished by how well she hid her fear. She believed that with a stroke of luck and a gust of will she'd cure me. I believed that I'd brought on my sickness. Why else would doctors want to tinker with my thoughts?

Mother rose and her bunched-up skirt tumbled toward the carpet. As she left with the tray, her skirt snagged on the corner of the bed. "Your bed has a nasty mind of its own," she said.

I shut my eyes and thought of what to do next: watch television or read the last chapter in *Don Quixote*. I'd never been bookish; give me fields and trees and dogs and games. But now I read and I read anything. I was no longer the gregarious one; Michael was. He'd shed his reticence and I'd gratefully slipped it over my head like a clean nightgown.

I woke up perspiring. Michael was sitting on the other bed, glancing through a stack of typed papers. What a good-looking brother he was. Someone, Rosa or Mother, had tidied up my room. Small daisies sprouted from a vase on my desk and the steam from the vaporizer tickled the back of several petals; a brown petal fell.

"Everyone's asking about you at school," Michael said. "Mister Rhipps gave me this: your review for the finals." He strode—such gallantry—to the vaporizer and put his hand over the steam. "Penn's coming over."

"I don't want him to see me in bed. I don't feel well." I thought of Penn and the time I'd skimmed through the parents' sex books, which unfortunately were few. I remembered the books excited me; and remembering, I felt embarrassed or even ashamed, as ashamed as when Mother had discovered I'd shaved my legs.

I said, "Sorry my friends are bothering you at school."

"They're not bothering me." His left foot fiddled with his right until his sneaker slipped off. His sneakers stank, a garden of spoiled tomatoes. He sat next to me and teased, "Where's Gina? Isn't she still your best friend?"

"Maybe she doesn't want to be with someone who's sick all the time."

"You're not sick all the time."

I remembered Gina the year before, doggedly following me into the girls' bathroom. Dizzy, I slid down, onto the dirty tiles. Gina stomped out in pursuit of Nurse Rachel. Then two classmates, Harley and Jennifer, came into the bathroom. Harley held my hand. As soon as buxom Nurse Rachel arrived, she asked me, "Are you upset over something, Cora?"

After Michael left, I had to get out of my immaculate room. It happened like that, a bolt: I was up, moving for the sake of movement. I felt weightless, as I do when I climb off a horse and there's no longer a horse to move. I went into my parents' bedroom.

My parents' bed had been made, its golden cover and leaf-embroidered pillows in place. Lately, I'd been sleeping there with Mother. Intricately carved moldings painted with golden leaves decorated the ceiling. No cigar boxes were on the dressers, no unironed trousers were limp over the chairs. A long desk stood opposite the windows and on it was a flier for a liquor store, announcing a sale. Father had highlighted a 1964 Château Haut-

Brion. He'd allowed me to taste several of his wines, but I couldn't remember whether I'd ever tasted this one.

Mother was humming in her bathroom, which adjoined a small dressing area. It seemed Mother and Father never dressed there at the same time. I went to her. She was combing her hair in deep strokes. She then pinned it back with tortoiseshell clips. I looked for gray strands but saw only red. "We're leaving in about forty minutes," she said and stroked my back. "Why don't you change?"

"I'm not depressed."

"This Doctor Wole seems to think talking to someone will help your sickness. Don't worry, Mum will be—"

"Can I borrow this sweater?" I pulled out a blue cardigan and several others fell to the floor.

"It'll be miles too big on you."

I took the gigantic sweater and slunk out of the bedroom and into my own. I brushed my hair. The friction brought on stunning electricity. I was a Medusa with albino snakes. I slid in my sock feet into the bathroom, pretending to care about what I wanted to do: cut my hair. Gina sometimes cut her own hair. Maybe it was Gina's mother who kept her away. Damn that woman. Maybe it was me. Damn me. And I gazed at myself: hell-bent but not doomed. A smooth round face stared back at me. I'd been allergic to the drug of choice: sulfur. Sulfur gave me headaches and rashes on my back. But cortisone, a precious steroid, had its cruelties; it made my bones brittle; at times it made me lose weight, other times gain weight. I pressed my pale face and watched the spot redden and swell up again. I concentrated on something other than me: *Les Fleurs du Mal*, a book I'd picked up by one of my favorite poets, Baudelaire. He called the reader a hypocrite; I appreciated his directness.

Dr. Georges sat poised with one hand on the desk, the other on the arm of her bright red-checked chair. Her furniture was meant to cheer up the patient, I thought. She had straight black hair and wore square horn-rimmed glasses, which slipped down her small parakeet nose whenever she moved her head. A generator or some such machine buzzed outside her dirty window. Three cigarette butts filled her ashtray. A series of smiling clown illustrations hung like banners on her white wall. I had this sharp desire to throw darts at any one of the clowns.

She said, "How are you feeling?" She adjusted her glasses.

"Great." I picked at my fingernail.

"Your mother tells me you've been feeling sad."

"Only when it hurts."

"How does it hurt?" She waited. "Does it hurt when missing school? Don't you miss your friends?"

I broke a fingernail off. Her fault.

"Do you have a boyfriend?" When met with silence again, she took off the cap of her pen. But she was no note-taker. "I see you still don't want to be here." She pushed the cap back on the pen.

"Do you smoke?" I asked and she nodded yes. "The ashes make me feel sick."

While she banged the steel ashtray against the trashcan, I thought she hadn't, after all, asked for me to come. "Doctor Georges, I want to go home," I said.

"Last time, your mother told me you were worried about missing so much school."

I slipped my foot out of my loafer and casually dipped my toes into an imaginary bucket of cold water. We didn't talk for a few minutes. Then I stood, the heel of my foot squishing down the back of my shoe.

"The session's not over yet," Dr. Georges said and rose halfway as if to grab me. She ripped off her glasses.

"I really feel sick now. Really." I didn't like her shoes; they were sparkling white, orthopedic.

As I opened the door, she sat back down, rubbed one gray eye and said, "You must be very angry that you have this disease. Are you angry?"

Well, well, I left that Dr. Georges rocking in her chair, wondering what the hell she was going to do with this angry, angry child. I needed no analyzing; Dr. Wole had no right to send me off to Dr. Georges. What exactly was she hoping to discover about my mind?

The waiting room was empty. I spotted Father pacing the hall.

He was a follower, I thought, flapping his slippers in the steps of a famous physician. He told me Mother had gone for a walk and would meet us outside. Suddenly he grabbed my hand and jerked me toward the elevators. He said, "Hospital elevators are terrible. To get out of here, you—"

"Dad, don't bring me back."

"Doctor Wole won't treat you if you don't come back."

"I hate him."

"Don't hate so much."

We picked Mother up in front of the hospital. While we'd been getting the car, she'd apparently gone back inside to chat with Dr. Georges. Mother said to Father, "The doctor says Cora should definitely return next week. Her reaction, she says, is only normal. But I care neither for Doctor Wole nor for his colleagues. He was outright rude last time; he asked Cora if she—"

"Don't!" I bit my lip.

"Wole's supposed to be the best there is," Father said.

"You are not addressing a committee, David. We will not go on recommendations. We have only Cora to go on."

I locked myself in my room. Lying motionless on my bed, I heard: "Penn the Great here."

Ah, the knight. I curtsied to myself in the mirror; I unlatched the door, grateful that Mother was finally asleep.

Penn pulled out the chair from the desk and drawled, "Just went to the roof. I told him we'd meet him up there."

Penn loved to talk on our roof. He marveled at the air, claimed it was cleaner. He said he preferred our roof to most: it was tiled, the water tower was sleek, the pigeons were few.

We snuck out by the upstairs door next to my bedroom. The stairwell smelled of ammonia and fresh paint. Only two flights to the top, and I, of course, started panting prematurely and fell with an exaggerated sigh against Penn. He kissed the back of my head. I didn't expect it; I didn't want it.

"Pity for the sick," I said and pretended I was holding a beggar's cup, which I rudely stuck out.

"I don't think so." His eyes darted to the rail, then back at me. He smacked together his full lips, lips the color of light chocolate mixed with strawberry. He started climbing again, two steps at a time.

"I wish everyone would stop worrying about me," I called up to him. I said softly, "I'm not worried." My arms and legs felt heavy, like feathers soaked in oil.

Penn held open the roof door for me. "Cora, I'm sorry you got so sick."

I'd never heard him sound so timid.

Michael was lying on a lounge chair, smoking a joint, his long legs hanging over the chair. Penn sat next to me. While his fingers rapped against the chair and while Michael stared at the sky, it happened, as it had many times before: so still, I imagined myself outside my body, playing with Penn's blond hair as he rubbed my flat chest, making me tease him more. I ventured away, buoyant now: a small balloon reaching the tower light of the Fifty-ninth Street Bridge. I was spinning upward in a tunnel of fluid, sniffing gaseous sulfur, noxious acid from the planets, white stars turning blue. Then I snapped out of the sky with a sneeze. I felt cold and tried to hide with a trembling hand what slipped out of my nose. How lucky I was, I thought, while casually rubbing my palm against the chair, lucky to be surrounded by these two guys.

"Want some?" Michael said and handed the joint to Penn. I wouldn't smoke, wouldn't dare weaken my mind. I liked to believe a sleeping pill weakened only my muscles.

"Penn's a star," Michael said. "He won the baseball game for us."

I then pictured Michael as a star. Worried I might not be well enough to see him perform his first role, I said, "When's the play again?"

" 'If we shadows have offended, Think but this, and all is mended, That you have but slumb'red here . . .' Next time, I'll be Lysander," Michael said.

I thought: Wouldn't it be swell if my sickness could be mended with a turn of a phrase? I was cold.

Penn said, "You're shivering, Cora."

We disbanded: Penn for home, Michael for his room, and I for Father.

The strong blue light of the television shone on his calm face. An empty cognac snifter stood on the table near his favorite chair. In his navy blue robe, he looked paler. He raised an arm to me, beckoning.

I said, "You're always fighting with Mom over my doctors."

"Doctors?" He smirked.

I perched myself at the desk and lazily doodled on a pad.

Father said, "Your principal called me yesterday. Mister Houseman's his name? He says you're missing so much school, he's concerned about some state law of attendance. He may not be able to pass you if you miss much more."

I broke the tip of the pencil. "I'm taking the finals. If I pass them, I'll be okay?"

"I think I convinced him of that."

"Mom knows about this? I need to know these things." I drew a distorted face.

"I don't worry about you." He yawned. "I'll be in Clarissa's room if you need me."

For weeks, Mother faithfully carried around her black book scribbled with each event of the day—how anemic I was, how much I'd eaten. And I kept my own little book. I hid it in my desk cabinet, knowing that Mother had cultivated her snooping skills and had managed to open the common padlock I'd use on my cabinet. Inside, I'd kept pot seeds, which she'd tossed down the toilet, no doubt unsure of what they were. I'd also kept private papers—not a diary, not my style—letters from Penn, from Clarissa, and old worn ones from Nanny. This time, I knew better than to trust a lock.

To baffle Mother, I invented a code to record the progress of my illness. The code consisted of several symbols: hats for the month of May, Roman numerals for the day, and an arrow pointing up for improvement, an arrow crossed or broken for an especially painful day:

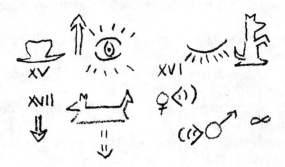

May 17: Fever, high. Father told Mother she's killing us all by keeping me out of a hospital.
May 19: Dr. W.'s replacement, a Dr. S., who has nothing to do with Dr. G.

Dr. Frederick Sanis, a five-foot-four stocky man with wispy yellow hair recommended ACTH shots, which, he explained, were a concentrated form of cortisone. He said a daily dosage was to be given intravenously, right away; he suggested I check into New York Hospital.

"Show me how to give her a shot," Mother said, rubbing together her *curandero* fingers. "I've given a shot before. I've just forgotten. We mustn't go to hospitals, not now."

He asked for an orange. While Mother fetched one, I talked to the doctor, whom I rather liked despite his desire to put me in a hospital. He asked me if I'd ever been to the Cabo Rojo lighthouse, outside Boquerón. I said no, that too many sights had gone unseen while we lived in Puerto Rico.

Mother soon scurried in, two oranges in hand and a mustache of perspiration on her upper lip.

"Pretend this is Cora's thigh," the doctor began and instructed her how to first pull out the plunger to see if any blood appeared. If it did, then Mother had found a vein. No use with a vein. The doctor told her to try injecting the orange. Mother's hand quivered. The orange fell to the carpet and rolled under my dresser.

"Let me try," I said and reached for the other orange.

Dr. Sanis squeezed the fruit. He said, "I tell you what: I'll visit you every morning. We'll exchange island stories and I'll give you your little shot." He rubbed the orange against his jacket and asked me if I wanted to eat it. Then he left me to Mother. "I'm not going to be kept back in school," I said to her. "Who said you were?" "Cut out the faking."

Now that I felt extremely ill, I recorded that I was better than I was. I routinely reviewed my hieroglyphics and reinterpreted them, making columns of new figures under one symbol to see how many meanings I could derive from it.

On the third day of shots, I surprised all my loved ones: I lost my appetite. No spice for this child. I nibbled at two toast-and-jam meals a day and memorized Baudelaire, sometimes in French, sometimes in English. My French was getting better. Yet who cared? I had no one to read to. At times I wanted to hear the words as Baudelaire would have heard them: "*Sans cesse à mes côtés s'agite le Démon; Il nage autour de moi comme un air impalpable.*" *

I paled from anemia; I thought it might be best to just keep sleeping, to pass off when no one noticed. I didn't feel morbid. I felt the demon.

One evening when Father was working late, Mother was lying on the other bed in my room, smoking a True cigarette. I challenged her: "Give me a smoke."

She said, "Haven't you noticed your father's always leaving? As if that will save the disaster he's begun up here. He doesn't need to go to Puerto Rico again on Friday."

"What disaster?"

With her cigarette she etched a V of smoke in the air. "I told him, I told your Uncle Stuart, too, not to buy these stores up

---

* "I come and go—the Demon tags along, hanging around me like the air I breathe."
Trans. Richard Howard.

here." A repeat of *Wild Kingdom* played on the screen. We watched gigantic alligators crawl out of swamps.

"Where's the store they just opened?" They had five new stores, in Port Washington, Larchmont, Northport . . . the location of the other two I'd forgotten.

"Syracuse, the biggest, but then again, I haven't seen it. Your father's wealth is due to me. Has he ever told you that? I remember when he used to scout for new stores. Sometimes he'd bring me along—this is way before you—and I'd tell him which spot I liked best. The store in Ponce was my choice." She laughed at an alligator's taped snout swinging against a cameraman.

When I was seven or eight, Father had driven me to a lot in Ponce. Isla had just blown up a shut-down doll factory. He told me a new Isla store would soon stand in its place. We parked in the middle of this inauspicious lot. Tires, cans, bottles, discarded food, were all scattered on the ground. Father said, That's where the store will stand. But you never know: someday, someone may start a fire by accident, or maybe on purpose, and our store will disappear, too.

Mother suddenly stood and waved me out of bed. "Best to change this blanket. It's too warm for this blanket."

"The blanket's fine." I glared at my bony ankles, white like Mother's. Her feet shuffled around the bed as she tossed the laundered lighter blanket.

"Don't just watch, Cora. Give me a hand."

But the familiar hood of hot air covered my head. I struck the night table with a heavy thud.

"Cora?" Her startled voice startled me. I vomited into my hands.

"Oh, why don't you go to the bathroom when you feel that coming on? My god, dear god, please, please, god." She muffled her crying with the blanket before either one of us thought to clean me up.

The fifth day of shots brought much-needed relief. I woke up feeling renewed at 3:00 A.M. and recorded in my notebook some new figures: combinations of alligators and dogs and horses. Then

I wandered, cloaked in that calm that comes with a few hours of sleep.

A dull light warmed the kitchen. I found the key to Father's wine cellar. I was prepared to commit some unforgivable act—breaking a wine bottle—so my disease could serve as a justified punishment. An expensive vintage would do nicely: shatter it near the incinerator. I opened the cellar door; I studied the rows of bottles, the white, the red. I held one, a Château Margaux, 1970. I knew how delicious this wine was. I gingerly laid it back down on the rack.

In the corner of the cellar, a battered black file cabinet stood, in which Father stored liquor store fliers and invoices. He usually locked it. I tugged at the handle and the drawer opened. The key was inside; the lock looked rusted. I leafed through the files and found an envelope from Father's office. Inside were photographs: Mother and I stood in one, me on the beach, sand running through my fingers. Another showed Clarissa and Michael and me in the pool when we were babies. The third photograph was of a woman. Her hand was raised as if she were waving. But the picture had been damaged and it was hard to see the woman's face. She wore a sleeveless dress. I held on to the photo and put the others back into the envelope and the file cabinet. I returned the cellar key to the kitchen.

A door creaked; I immediately stuck the photo in my underwear. Father's footsteps were hushed by his leather slippers, worn thin at the toe. "I see someone else can't sleep," he said. "I was just going to get some port."

The photograph scraped hard against my skin as I walked to the den. Father came in. Before he had a chance to sit down, I said, "Mom had me go into your cellar the other day to get a price list. When I was looking for it, I found a bunch of photographs. There's one I've never seen before. You know the picture?"

He turned on the television set. "Don't go into my things, honey. I don't go into yours." He turned up the volume. He wiped a drop of port that had dribbled along his chin.

"I'll get the photo."

"Forget about it."

I said, "Aren't you wondering which picture I'm talking about?"

He said, "Cora, she's an old friend, an old girlfriend, if that's what you want to know. Now let me watch my program."

The next morning, he flew to Puerto Rico.

Michael tested me for the finals. He was sprawled on the other bed, book in hand, eating a cookie. He'd just had his hair cut and pale skin outlined the new cut. I'd made it a point to be in jeans and a shirt; I'd made it a point to make my much-hated bed.

Michael sucked, a nasty habit, on a cookie edge until it softened. "Okay, Thoreau's dates," he said.

"Eighteen seventeen. Died 1862."

He peered up, eyelids like hoods. "I'll read a passage and you tell me who it is. 'In the absence of man, we turn to nature, which stands next. In the divine order, intellect is primary—' "

I said Emerson. He dropped the book and patted his neck as if surprised he could feel it. He was getting up to leave when he said, "They're crazy if they don't let you pass."

"Everyone thinks everyone's crazy." I wanted to elaborate: They made me go to a psychiatrist to find out why I make myself bleed. Then I wanted to blurt out: I don't believe in God anymore and I'm not at all disappointed about that. But I only reached for the mottled photograph I'd tucked under the typewriter. I said, "Look what I found last night."

He studied it. "Who is it?"

"An old girlfriend of Dad's. Kind of neat, huh—a part of him we don't know."

"I read about the Northport store in the paper. It's closing down," Michael said and tossed the photo on the desk.

The day of the finals, the schoolyard was completely shaded. Three wooden benches stood empty and clean. Mother, wearing a navy linen pants suit, piloted me by the hand to the gate. I shook her grip loose. Gina, Harley and Kim—Kim I barely knew—all whispered near the door, Kim holding a piece of paper in her hands. Mother left, and Gina, in bright black and red checks, gaily bounced up to me.

"It's so good to see you," she said.

"I should get inside." I walked ahead, chin up, and a swatch of black and red checks raced across my vision.

"Wait." Perky Gina stood in front of me, hugging her school-bag. "Good luck."

Kim said hello, her slender hands still clutching a piece of paper.

"You look good," Harley offered and gripped my arm. "How are you?"

"Better," I said to perky Gina and humble Harley.

Kim said, "Which tests are you taking? History and math? We already took them. Maybe they're the same." She positioned herself behind Harley. Careful, careful Kim.

"I'm taking history, English," I said.

"If it's the same history we took, there's nothing on the Transcendentalists," Gina said and brought out of her schoolbag a wad of aluminum foil.

Kim eyed her letter and glanced up at me. "Remember AC?"

The few times Kim and I had chatted, she spoke only of AC Humbolt, a heavyset British boy in our class, with, rumor spread, a plush blond chest.

"Are you dating him?" I said and checked my watch. I didn't want to be late for the test.

"I am," she sighed and twirled halfway around. "I'm meeting him tonight on Park Avenue."

Gina kissed me on the cheek, pressing in my moist hand the crumpled foil. Kim, her dark bangs skimming her plucked eyebrows, stepped closer to me. "You're not in pain anymore, are you?" Peppermint was on her breath.

I pushed open the thick glass doors. Up the weathered blue stairs to the third floor I ran. I rushed and thought of missed parties, love notes and phone calls after twelve. The janitor was on the third floor, mopping near the lockers. I opened the foil Gina had given me. Inside was a large yellow tooth, Egg's best apple-biting tooth. Egg, Gina's dead white mare; the tooth, Gina's rabbit foot. I thought it was stunning, so cubic and gritty. I walked to the assigned room, rapidly squeezing the tooth in my hand. I thought of alligators and how they water-danced, slamming their tails and heads against the water when courting, agitating the swamp with their tense muscles. I heard the janitor slosh water into the pail. Alligators bellowed when mating. And what a knack: to effortlessly rip off an arm, to swallow muscle and skin, the warm meat spicing up their cold blood.

I took a sleeping pill when I got home. By nine, the small yellow pill had sufficiently deadened my senses. I heard the downstairs door bang twice, the dog yap and footsteps like clods of dirt hitting the stairs. My door swung open. Father came in, dropping his wrinkled damp raincoat and briefcase on the carpet. "Well?"

"Just two more tests to go," I said.

"I'm so happy for you—you've no idea. I couldn't stop thinking about you on the plane." He kissed me, wine on his breath, but he wasn't drunk. Plunging his hands into his pockets, he strolled to the windows, just speckled with rain. He was a young father, I thought, as he smoothed back his thinning bluish-black hair. He picked up a Doors cassette from my desk, read the list of songs aloud. I scraped at the enamel of the night table and got a good chunk of wood under my fingernail.

Father went to get some cognac.

I thought of Gina and Harley, Kim and AC, with his luscious brassy hair, and a sadness tingled through me, a self-pity really, but as present as if Mother were squeezing a sopping towel over my head. How could I let Penn touch me again after so many doctors prodded at me? I picked the wood chip from my nail, flicked it across the room. I took my notebook from my cabinet and opened it to a blank page. A most notable notebook.

What did Harley and Kim talk about at night? How many times had Gina phoned when I first became ill? I felt so inflamed and ruined, I hung up in a snap. I thought I was superior to Gina, to Harley, to Kim: I had endured steady pain and occasional humiliation.

Feeling too light-headed, I didn't hide the notebook when Father walked in with a cognac. He said, "You're going to school, tomorrow, aren't you?"

"School's just about over." I turned on the television and then glanced back at Father, whose fingers were stuck in my notebook. He set the cognac on the carpet and held up a page. I didn't really mind that he read all my gibberish. My body felt like putty.

He said, "Looks funny, like a children's book."

"A children's book?" I said. The purpose of the book? Symbols, the narrative of an incomprehensible code: conveying nothing.

As I rose to look at the notebook with him, I tipped the snifter with my foot. Father's hand swept up the glass. I, luxuriating in my daze, strolled into the bathroom for a washcloth. Oh, I'd keep it all clean for Mother.

"I noticed that picture's gone," he said.

"You can have it back." I crouched down to soak up the cognac. Mother would have a fit. She'd yell at him for drinking in my room.

"The picture doesn't matter, Cora. When you get to be my age, there are people you'll remember as if they belonged to someone else's past and not your own. But, Cora, I've never loved anyone the way I love you." He sounded as if he'd never said it before—when was the last time?—and then, as if expected to, he looked away.

I vigorously rubbed the spot. I recognized that he was hurt. How was I to help him? I said, "Where's the woman now?"

"She died." Gently, so gently, he patted my head—I almost didn't feel it. He whispered, "I think your old dad's sleepy."

Cliffs

Lee was my boyfriend. In April, he came with me to Bat Island. Cora and Michael were already there. We'd had the house for a few years. We went to it every spring. I was on my break, in my last semester at Middlebury College. Lee had taken a few days off from work. He skipped college to learn his father's business: a supplier of worms and crabs for bait and tackle stores. He was twenty-three, I was twenty-one. He acted older than his age. And I liked that.

I'd met him my sophomore year at a party in New York City. On our first date, we took a train to Coney Island. We rode the Cyclone, a roller coaster, four times in a row. Neither of us screamed. Later, we slept together at his parents' apartment. They lived at 44 Gramercy Park. Lee told me, "They moved into that apartment because when they got married, it was one of the only buildings in the neighborhood that let in Jews."

Gramercy Park itself takes up a city block. It has a gate around it. Only the people who live in the neighborhood can get a key to the park. They pay for the key. The night Lee and I went to the park, no one was there. We made love on a bench. I remember that afterward I walked to the gate. Lee followed me. He ran the park key up my back. At that moment, I thought I'd marry him; he knew what I wanted. I'd been with enough guys to feel sure of that.

Now he was leaning over me. He peered out the window of the seaplane. He pointed to the island and said, "It looks like a butterfly."

I agreed: the smaller side, to the east, gave the illusion of flight. I told him the bats lived there. I showed him the three peninsulas called the Fingers, on the lower tip of the eastern side. I told him Wing Bridge connected the two sides of the island. I said, "The house is shaped like a barbell. You'll sleep in the den, at one end. I'll be at the other end, sleeping with Cora."

He said, "We'll be sleeping in balance, architecturally. Yin-Yang theory. That'll help us sleep apart."

The next day, Lee and I were sitting in the living room. It was early afternoon. We'd decided we'd announce our engagement at dinner. Mom was talking to us about flying. She said she'd never had a good experience on an airplane.

Michael was prying off the back panel of a radio. Around his wrist he wore several braided strings of leather. He looked younger than sixteen.

Mom sat at the chess table. She said, "Martha told me a lovely story about how the Fingers got their name." Martha Megran lived on the island. She ran a grocery store. "There was a captain," Mom told us, "and he had three fingers on one hand. His wife had died of some fever and he was mad with grief and he began hallucinating—"

Dad came into the room. He carried a book. One of Bach's partitas for violin played from inside the den. "Which myth is this?" Dad said. He shuffled into the kitchen.

Mom waited until he was out of sight. Then she said, "One

day, the ship came to Bat Island. The captain had lost all sense of time and stayed in his cabin. He told the crew to build a port for his wife and to name it after her. But the men got lazy. They sailed a few hundred yards every few weeks, anchored in another spot on Bat Island—let's see—then, yes, they dug a small harbor, like a private port. Then one day, the captain came on deck for a bit of air, and he saw that the harbors formed three fingers out of the shoreline. Here was his gift to his wife: his hand, reaching for her."

I was quiet. Lee said, "That's the kind of gift I'd make for you, Clarissa, the kind the whole world can see." Michael laughed a little. Cora scoffed and stared at her feet. Dad, a piece of bread in hand, came into the living room.

Mom said, "Watch for crumbs, please. We don't have a maid." She got up to find more cigarettes.

Dad sat next to me on the couch.

"I fixed the radio," Michael said to him. "A wire was cut. How could that have happened?"

Lee said, "We have an important announcement. We're getting married."

I grabbed his elbow. I said, "Lee."

"Where's the champagne?" Dad said. Then he hugged me.

Cora rushed to the kitchen to fetch a bottle.

I tried to hide my anger with Lee for surprising me. I said to Mom, "We're going to wait till after graduation, of course."

Mom walked toward the terrace. She said, "I didn't expect this." She slid open the terrace door.

Mom had been in her bedroom for over an hour before I decided to go in. I found her in the bathroom. "But you're not even undressed," I said. The shower was running. Steam fogged the mirror. "I thought you liked Lee."

She didn't answer. She stepped under the water. Through the glass doors, I watched her hair straighten. Her skirt and blouse clung to her body.

I opened the shower door. I said, "Please talk to me."

She shut off the water and stepped onto the bath rug. "Why

didn't *you* talk to *me?* How could you keep something like this from me?" She then said she wanted to be left alone. As I walked out, I glanced at myself in the mirror. I was sucking in my cheeks, as Mom sometimes did.

I went to Dad in the den. He said to me, "Don't worry so much. It's only normal. You're her first."

Lee said, "I don't know, David." Lee liked to call people by their first name. "Maybe Clarissa should have made the announcement."

"Julia, Julia." Dad said. He shook his head as Mom walked by. She'd changed into a dry dress. She seemed oblivious of us and was quickly out the door. He put the newspaper down. "Let's try our luck fishing," he said to me. "I've got the butterfish and sand eels in the car."

I said, "Don't you think you should talk to Mom?"

Dad looked at Lee and said, "She stopped talking to me some time ago."

To get to the beach, Lee and I walked north. There was one road. It went along the cliffs and led to Wing Bridge. Lee took my hand.

I said, "We did have a deal: we were going to announce the engagement at dinner."

He picked me up and kissed me. "I was too excited about it. We're going to do so much together and we're going to do it right. Look, if your mom wasn't pleased then, she wouldn't have been pleased later. Maybe she's upset about something else. It's hard to say with your parents."

"You're right," I said and thought of his parents. They played tennis on weekends. They took trips. When they fought, his mother hit his father on the arm. I'd once pointed out to Lee that his parents made a good couple. And he'd said, "They're in their own world. If they ever stepped out of it, their marriage would fall apart."

We passed some lemon trees and Lee picked a lemon off one. The road sloped toward the bridge. The smell of seaweed was getting stronger.

Lee said, "I love it here, Clarissa. It's one of the few times I don't feel guilty about missing work. Let's check out the Fingers later."

I spotted Dad's Jeep parked on the side of the road. Dad, Michael and Cora were on the bank under the bridge. I wondered where Mom was.

"Looks like they're ready to fish," Lee said. "I used to love fishing with my father. I used to admire him like hell. I told you: he was my best friend through high school. But now I see it's better not to be too much like him."

I said, "Sometimes your father acts younger than you do." When we'd first met, Lee had told me that as a little boy he'd never wanted brothers or sisters. He thought he was lucky to have his father all to himself.

His father's name was Edward. Edward liked to drink with the men who drove his company trucks. He liked to play cards with his customers. Lee disapproved. He tried to keep to schedule, while Edward joked that maybe one day his son should take over, so Edward could enjoy himself again. I thought of Edward's warehouse. It used to be a warehouse for meat. The sign above the front door read: BERRYMAN & SON: FRESH BAIT. Lee said it was his idea to add "& Son." The first time I'd gone there, Lee took me into a gigantic refrigerator. I saw worms packed in boxes of seaweed. I saw sand eels, squid, butterfish and herring in bags in a freezer. Lee told me of a trick he'd learned from his father: when worms started to die, Lee mixed fresh worms into the box. His father couldn't support his wife and Lee on his business alone. Lee's mother seemed to bring in much of the family income. She was an accountant. I knew little about her. She was polite to me but not warm. Lee said she was warm only to Edward.

"I'll tell you something funny, Clarissa," Lee said when we got to the bridge. "But don't laugh, okay? Once, I had this green crab—"

"I don't want to hear this, do I?"

"I was about six. My father took me on a tour of the company. Anyway, a green crab comes right up to my foot and I took it

home and built it a sand castle in a guinea pig cage. But it got
out; it ran away. I felt close to this stupid crab."

I stared at him. He was sexy. He had a high forehead and curly
hair, long enough to reach his shoulders. In the sun, his eyes
turned from brown to orange. I said, "The wonderful little things
I still have to learn about you."

He smiled. "I remember that crab very well," he said, and I
laughed.

We went under the bridge and said hello to Dad. An old man
walked toward us. He stopped near Cora. Dad turned to him,
and the man crossed the bridge, going east. He had a cane
hooked around his neck. In each hand he carried a coconut. He
smelled of whiskey. I'd seen him once or twice in town. Martha
Megran had told me he was her grandfather. He limped around
the island all day. Now he was hitting two coconuts together. He
said, "David Lyon. Merry fishing."

Dad said to me, "Do I know that man?"

There's no beach on the east side of the island. So Lee and I
didn't cross the bridge. We walked south. At the far end of the
beach, two boys were throwing a ball. A woman shouted at the
boys. A man rested in the sun. And there was Mom, walking.
She was kicking the sand. The man tipped up his glasses as she
passed him.

Lee and I lay in the sun. I thought of having to go to work. But
where? I aimed to make money. I wanted to spend it as I pleased.
I thought earning a lot of money would keep me independent of
Lee. I didn't want to end up like my mother: dependent on my
father.

I'd studied art history in college for my first two semesters,
switched over to psychology, then to education, then back to art
history for my last semester. I'd told myself I should get a job as
an assistant in an art gallery. But I didn't know much about the
art world. I soon decided it would take too long to make a lot of
money working for a gallery, unless I owned it. My father had
suggested I consider a job as an account executive in advertising.

He said I'd become an expert in marketing and demographics. I'd, for the most part, rely on other people's decisions. I'd use facts to help sell ideas to my clients. I thought I could do that: I'd be charming, I'd put on airs. Cora had once said to me, "Your pretensions are almost becoming."

Mom was at the far end of the beach. There the rocks trapped the ocean water and turned it into pools. She was climbing over the rocks to the pools. She took off her sundress. She wore an old-fashioned bathing suit, the kind with a skirt. She stepped into one pool and didn't see that the man stared.

I left Lee on the beach. He was sleeping.

I went into the ocean. Under water, opening my eyes, I tried to think of something about Lee I didn't like. Perhaps it'd be the same thing Mom didn't like. Lee asked little of others. He also preferred if others asked little of him. And he pretended to know about things he knew nothing about: a star had such and such concentration of carbon dioxide and nitrogen. At times that made him witty. He believed he'd be successful one day. I believed he'd always *try* to be a success. I wanted Mom to have as much faith in him as I did. I took off the bottom of my bikini. Then I slipped off the top. I swam close to the sand. The water turned colder as I swam deeper. The salt began stinging my eyes. I squirmed back into the suit and swam ashore.

I walked toward Mom. I put my foot on a rock by a pool.

She was gathering her hair on top of her head. She reminded me of Cora. She looked down at the water. She reminded me of Michael, double-checking whether or not he had his sneakers tied. I couldn't see myself in her.

"I haven't been well Clarissa," she said, cupping water in her hands. "I have a lot on my mind. Now, tell me how much you love Lee."

It was later that same night. Lee and I were at the Fingers, talking about our families. Lee said, "My mother's a very good accountant. Unlike my dad, she's all business. I take after her. I'd do anything for a profit. I'd even be a parasite."

"Me, too. We're exemplary capitalists."

"Models of virtue," he said and unwrapped a bottle of wine from a towel.

The forest was behind us. I could hear the wind blowing through the trees. The wind was loud: it sounded as though bits of glass were flying onto a floor. A bat passed overhead. I squealed and Lee hushed me.

I said, "My mother couldn't wait to come here. She showed me a Polaroid of the house and said, 'How wonderful: we'll be in the middle of nowhere.' She was beginning to hate Puerto Rico. She called the people filthy. Maybe she was hoping this island would make Dad happy, though he seems far from happy to me. My mother's happy just having him in mind. I'm like her in that way. I don't do a thing without having you in mind."

"You're about as selfless as I am," he said. "Not that that's a bad way to be. If you always act in the interest of others, you may forget who you are." I couldn't tell whether or not he was joking. He wasn't smiling.

I heard a scraping noise. We both turned. The old man we'd seen earlier was coming out of the forest. He still had his cane hooked around his neck. He drew the brush apart. A branch was stuck to the back of his shirt.

"You're the Lyons," he said. "Hey, I know everyone around here. I knew Mitchell Willet before he owned the island. Those were the days: he used to bring in musicians on the weekends. A little calypso," he said and wiggled his hips. "A little Beethoven . . ." He slipped a pint of rum out of a baggy pocket. He offered us rum. I said no. He twisted the cap off. "It's a good night to be watching bats. Did you know that in some countries they eat bats? Yep, you can find a big bat next to the steaks in the frozen meat section of the supermarket."

Lee said, "I'm Lee Berryman, this is Clarissa Lyon."

"And I'm Terrence Huston," he said and held out his hand. Lee shook it. Terrence put the rum bottle back in his pocket. He said, patting his pocket, "I live here alone. My daughter died recently. Her name was Tanya Huston. She fell off a cliff."

"I'm sorry," I said. I wanted to leave.

Terrence sneezed. He took a handkerchief from his shirt pocket. He blew his nose and then said, "I'm not really alone, I suppose. Tanya had a child. Her name's Martha. Martha has a store in town. I'm sure you know it." He laughed. He hit his cane against a tree. "I helped Martha start her store. I know about these things. . . . I used to be a banker. I used to be well-respected. But—" He stopped. He hit his cane against the ground and said, "David Lyon doesn't talk to me. That I don't understand." He patted the ground near the water and then dug a hole. He scooped up wet dirt. Worms poked out of the mound of dirt. "Your father, Clarissa, he needs these if he's going to catch any fish on this island."

Lee said, "Those worms won't do the trick."

Terrence ignored him. He was looking at the water.

We said good night to him and went back to the Jeep.

"He's a fool," I said.

Lee said, "More like a heartfelt salesman, if you ask me."

It was June, two days before my wedding. Cora and I were strolling along the beach. She said, "I don't want to be sick again, but I can't get used to being healthy."

"School will be good for you," I told her. "You'll be on your own." She'd been accepted at the University of Chicago.

She said, "Too many people in school."

A golden retriever leapt up to us and then hurried into the water. Cora searched for a stick. She hurled the stick at the dog. The dog loped back to Cora. Again, Cora threw the stick. "Whose dog?" she said.

"Why don't you try to get together with Evan?" Evan Wiston was the son of Rhia Wiston. She lived down the road from us. She ran a restaurant on the island. Evan had told me he wanted to ask Cora out. I wanted her to have someone to talk to, outside of our family.

"Why is a guy always the answer to everything for you? First Allen, then Kevin, then there was . . . ? Was there a Tad somewhere?"

"Good of you to keep track. So who *do* you like?"

"I like Penn," she said.

"Penn has a girlfriend."

"Swell," she said, "swell." She buried her foot in the sand.
"Dad has two stuffed suitcases in his closet."

"Two?"

The dog was shaking himself. He sprayed us with water.

Lee and I had a small wedding. Mom twisted yellow and white roses in vines around the trees. She put rose topiaries on the terrace. Except for Mitchell Willet, we invited only our families. A violinist, a cellist and a pianist played at the reception. After an hour or so, Lee told them to stop playing classical. He told them to play jazz.

"Do I look different?" he said to me. He tugged on his lapels. "After you marry, your hormones alter and make you look younger. It's a fact."

"The facts according to Lee," I said and then overheard Lee's mother, Terry, say to Dad: "I never took my husband's business seriously until Lee got involved with it. My husband, I'm sorry to say, never took it seriously. He's never really been a model for Lee. He adores Lee, but he's . . . well, you understand my meaning."

Dad told Terry how much he respected Lee's business sense.

I went to talk to Mitchell Willet. He wore a white tuxedo and a pocket watch. Mom was standing next to him. She was waving her hands in the air to emphasize a story she was telling. Mitchell Willet complimented me on my dress. Then he said, "I couldn't bring your wedding present. Would you drop by tonight to pick it up?"

Mom said, "It sounds very special." She danced by herself for a minute.

Willet placed his hand on her waist. He said to me, "The happier marriages never settle into what they are expected to be."

The doorbell rang. Lee and I answered it. Terrence stood outside. He hadn't been invited. One of the buttonholes of his suit was torn. He seemed sober and held a small gift. He said, "I'm not here to stay." He lifted the gift.

"Stay," Lee said.

Dad hurried over to us.

Terrence said, "I've got to be going—" But Lee insisted he stay and then led him outside to the party.

Dad flicked his upper lip with his forefinger. He said, "You invite who you want." He disappeared into the den.

I followed him. In the den, he stood reaching for a box of Cuban cigars. He tore the seal on the box. "What is it, sweetheart?" He selected the third cigar, smelled it from one end to the other. He sounded so calm. He sounded as if he were the most contented married man in the world. I thought of his suitcases in the closet. I said, "How long did you think you could keep your leaving a secret?"

He paced, holding the cigar like a pencil. He stopped pacing. "Is now the time? At your wedding?"

I said, "Okay, you won't talk about it." I looked at the bookshelf. He had many books but only a few subjects: Ballet, Business, Israel, French Cooking, Baseball. I looked out the terrace door. I thought we were lucky that every room had a terrace. My family always had an exit at hand. I'd already made my exit, I thought, and watched Lee. He was talking to his mother. Next to him, Terrence was showing Michael the steps of the merengue.

It took Lee and me almost a half hour to get to Mitchell Willet's house. We could see the town from the road. The town is shaped like a horseshoe. One side of the horseshoe has the bat shop, Martha Megran's general store, the coffee shop and pharmacy, both run by a Cruzan named Tack, and then there's Rhia Wiston's restaurant. The hotel, the bank and post office, the souvenir store, are all on the other side. The hotel is full on holidays and has a parking lot for six cars.

I said, "The island used to be completely private. One man lived here."

"And he lost someone he loved," Lee said.

Mom would say that, I thought. "No, he didn't. He was a scientist. He studied bats and set so many traps in the caves that the bats flew away. So the man left. Discouraged, I guess."

"I don't think I could feel any better than I do right now," Lee said as we came to Willet's cottage.

The cottage had vines covering its walls. Blue and white curtains hung in the windows. Large torches, stuck in the ground, turned the yard and entranceway a bright yellow. Willet opened the door before we arrived at the doorstep. Inside, the house was stark. A white cockatoo stood in a cage by the kitchen.

Lee settled into an armchair. He leaned back, and the chair flipped into a lounger. He laughed and said, "Top choice: a superb reading chair." I stood behind the chair.

Willet left for the kitchen and returned with some sherry. "Pot Hammer used to live here," he said. He handed us the sherry.

I said to Lee, "The guy who scared off the bats."

"He was nicknamed Pot," Willet said, "because he left behind the most amazing chamber pots. That very kitchen used to be his bat laboratory. And off to the left there's a breakfast room, which he used as a study. Now come into the study."

In the study, there was a kitten, cleaning itself. Lee picked it up.

"It's an Abyssinian," Willet said. He took the cat from Lee. "I give you an Abyssinian for a reason. There's a bit of history involved." He opened a cabinet under the bookshelves. He took out some posters. He unrolled them and rattled through the papers. Showing us one, he said, "Here we go: Before you lived in your house, a man named Arthur Morris lived there. From '62 through '69. He had dozens of Abyssinians, and now"—he pointed to our names on the paper—"you're on the map with your very own."

How many bits of history did he know about? His chart made it seem as if he'd known all the people who had once lived on the island. The paper showed Terrence Huston in the left-hand corner, a date printed under his name. What about his child? I said, "I thought Terrence had a daughter and Martha was his granddaughter."

"Oh, Huston!" Willet said. "He's a good man. He used to be very successful. When he retired, he bought himself the Ossining place in '71. You see here," he said, rattling the paper again. "Ossining. But Huston's peculiar: he believes he once had a daughter by the name of Tanya, who fell off a cliff. Who's hurt by his lie?"

Lee said, petting the cat, "He's certainly not helped by it."

"Listen, it's not a dishonorable thing; he's not a dishonorable man," Willet said. "Maybe it's even good because Martha is willing to go along with him; she loves him like a father. She's a deep soul. She reminds me of your mother: very rooted in family." He took the cat from Lee and said, "Do you like cats?"

We left for our honeymoon the next morning. Michael drove us to the marina. Alfonso Menudo's boat was docked there, waiting for us. I thought of Dad leaving Mom. Would he live on Bat Island? And how would Mom handle her time? I felt neither sad nor relieved. I felt indifferent, as if they were someone else's parents.

Lee said, "Terrence didn't seem like the kind of guy who'd go around telling stories so you'd pity him. I don't understand people who make up a life just because they don't like how they've lived their own."

"And you're so honest," I said. "You mix dead worms with live ones."

Lee looked to the cliffs.

I told him I was sorry. Then I said, "I feel bad for Terrence. He's alone. He's a drunk. He's typical."

Michael said, "Tomorrow you'll both wake up in Saint Croix." He parked the car and picked up our two suitcases. He started whistling.

Alfonso Menudo's boat bumped and creaked against the dock. Michael scampered onto the boat. He greeted a captain we'd never met. Lee walked up to the bow.

Michael said to me, "You're feeling very good about starting a life of your own." He hugged me, a long hug for Michael, I thought. Then he left.

I went to Lee. He was tearing matches out of a matchbook and dropping them into the water. "I am sorry," I said. "Why stay angry with me? Terrence Huston means nothing to us."

"I'm not angry." He dropped the matchbook into the water. He said, "I don't want to be."

Packing for Winter

A few months after our honeymoon, Edward gave Lee his business. Then Lee and I found a two-bedroom apartment on Sixty-fifth Street, off First Avenue. We spent neither the time nor the money to furnish it. We were fifteen blocks north of my mother. My father was living on Bat Island for a few months. Then he planned on returning to Puerto Rico to live.

I found a job as a junior account executive in a large ad agency. I worked late. Lee worked later. He had three basic routes: one in each of the five boroughs, one on the south shore of Long Island and one in New Jersey. He sold to over two hundred stores. Edward used to get bait from the boats at Shinnecock, Montauk and Freeport. He used to buy the fish that hadn't been sold at the Fulton Market. But Lee never went to Fulton Street. Instead, he went to the docks. He charmed the boat owners and gave them souvenirs: compasses and fishing caps with *Berryman Bait* printed on them. He bargained with them, too. One night, he invited a boat owner to dinner. The boat owner imitated Lee. He crossed his arms at his chest and said to me, "Give me the plump, fresh stuff." The boat owner also said: "What a difference from Edward."

Lee's day began before mine. By 5:30 A.M., he was at the warehouse, training salesmen. Edward had relied on the same three guys for years. But Lee hired new people. I learned how much he believed in his workers. I admired what I learned of Lee. He was not yet twenty-five. We were a successful young couple, a little out of sync.

At night, I tried to talk to him about his work. I liked to talk about my own. I thought my job was easy, dealing in small space ads. But to impress Lee, I'd say, "I'm learning so much." He'd sit on the couch, switch on the television and say about his own day, "Work is fine." He took two showers every night, one when he got home, one before he went to bed. Ruby, our cat, wrapped around his legs.

I never said anything about the showers or about the smell from the bait. But one evening, I'd had an unsuccessful client meeting. Lee had brought home a piece of crab shell in the sole of his shoe. I stepped on it. I shouted at him: Be considerate. He had nothing to apologize for, he told me. Days later, he said, "Don't condescend to me when it comes to my work."

It was a Sunday morning. I wanted to sleep late. Lee got up early. He told me the morning was unusually warm for November; he was going for a walk. I sat in bed, wondering where he'd go. To work? to a coffee shop? or just across town and back? I got up after he'd left. I went through his briefcase. There were a lot of legal papers. I didn't read them.

Out the window, I saw how white the sky was. A thin cloud lay across the sun. The starkness of the sky reminded me of a beach in Puerto Rico and I felt steady for the moment. I felt good. The emptiness of the apartment wasn't even bothering me. I cleaned up.

Lee came home an hour or two later. I asked him where he'd been.

He said, "I headed across town and stopped to watch this card game. You know those cardplayers who sucker in people on the street and then rip them off? There's a dealer and there are his shills. They make it look like you can win. So I notice this young guy inching closer and closer to the game. He puts down fifty dollars and plays. He loses, of course. Then I hear him say to the dealer that he'll be right back. I follow him. The young guy goes straight to his car, takes out some money from the glove compartment and I go up to him and tell him there's no way he can win the game. He looks surprised. Then, after a few minutes, he says, Why do you care? I tell him that these guys steal from people. And he says, So you don't work with them? He starts to laugh. Then he shows me the money he took out of his car. He had three hundred dollars to bet with. He looks so young, Clarissa, and I'm wondering if he's a serious gambler or something, but I'm guessing he just doesn't know better. Then he tells me he's very grateful to me. He shakes my hand and leaves. It's a shame how conditioned people are: I mean they're scared to help each other; they're scared to even be helped."

"How do you know he didn't go back to the card game later?" I asked.

Lee started walking toward the kitchen. He said, "That's not the point of the story."

One December night, Lee came home late. He kept on his coat and then told me about work. He said the president of Packer Fish & Bait Corporation, a large distributor in Virginia, wanted to expand to the northeast. The president had offered to buy Lee's business. Lee wanted to sell. He said, "My father can't believe I'm getting rid of the place after he just gave it to me."

"Your father's had the business for over thirty years. Shouldn't you talk to a lawyer about this?"

"A lawyer is working on a contract as we speak," Lee said.

I went into the kitchen to boil water for tea. Like Mom, I enjoyed tea in the early and late evening. On my way back, I said, "Is it a fair price?"

"Of course." He took off his coat. "I'll make dinner."

I said, "Where will you work?"

"Please, Rissa, I've been arguing with my father all afternoon. I'll tell you more when I know more." He picked up the cat and left his coat on the couch. On his way to the kitchen, he said, "Your mother called me at the office. She couldn't get you at work. She says Rosa's very sick."

Saturday, I went to Mom's to see Rosa. Rosa was sleeping when I got there. Michael was in the kitchen. He was reading A. C. Bradley's *Shakespearean Tragedy*. His new role was Shylock in *The Merchant of Venice* for the Shakespeare Festival at his school.

I sat at the breakfast table and thought of Lee. I felt as if he were living without me. He'd never think to ask my opinion on selling the business. And he seemed to have no feeling about his decision. I said to Michael, "I'm not sure Lee knows what he's doing."

"I'm sure he's going to make a lot of money," Michael said, still reading.

"In the first few months, it was all great, like camp." I tried to sound childish.

"It?"

"Marriage. It was like camp, a cultural camp."

"You never went to any camp."

"Lee and I used to go to movies, plays, concerts. Now it's all very serious; it's all so cold."

Mom walked in. She wore a silk caftan with a band around it. I said, "You look like a Japanese maiden."

She didn't respond. She asked Michael to help her move Rosa's blankets into the den.

Michael said, "Why don't you leave her alone?"

"Why don't you do what I ask?" Mom said. "As it is, my day's been ruined. I was supposed to meet with the lawyer to talk about your father's abandoning me without notice, and then the lawyer canceled. At least I got the doctor to make a house call for Rosa; he's coming Monday, at ten. He couldn't come today and Rosa refuses to go to him. I suppose she can't feel too bad. Monday at ten." She went to write that down.

"I have a rehearsal at six," Michael said. "It'll be a late night."

"You'll have to miss it. I need help here," Mom said.

"I wasn't asking you if I could go." He sounded matter-of-fact.

She looked angry but said without yelling, "If you go tonight, go, but then don't come home."

He stood and spilled a drop of coffee on the tile. I wiped it up after he left.

"Don't clean up after him," Mom said. "This whole household cleans up after him. *I* clean up after everyone."

"Maybe you should get a job."

"Oh, yes, Clarissa, you're quick to give advice when it's convenient for you, aren't you? What about what's convenient for me? When I'd like a little help, you and your brother are never around. When my mother needed me, I was there. And after she died, I worked. I had to. I lied about my age and got a job in a clothing factory. I didn't need a glorious college education. I have a job. I work for this family and I'm not one bit ashamed of it."

In the afternoon, Lee and Ruby, both bundled up, strutted into the apartment together. Lee carried the litter pan and litter in a shopping bag. He said, "It seems we're here so much, I thought Ruby would like to come."

"Tell me I'm here too much. Don't bring the cat to tell me."

He looked at Ruby, who rubbed her side against the wall. "It's just too cold to be anywhere alone." He put his arms around my waist. "I'm very happy about this deal."

"Rosa looks terrible."

"I brought the cat for Rosa. She said she wanted to see her." Then he told me that he and his lawyer had almost finished their work. He said, "I was thinking that there'd never be a shortage of worms in this world. And in that way, my father's work was very safe; a safe business can't always guarantee growth."

"I can't say I ever thought of that."

"No, I guess you wouldn't have." He sounded tired.

Mom carried in a pitcher of water and a glass. "Lee Nigel, you've brought a four-legged creature into my home."

He said, "I apologize. I assumed my cat would be as welcome as I am. Cats are adaptable creatures. If only we could be as flexible as they are."

Rosa came in, wearing a shawl over her robe. She said to Lee, "*Cariño*, you look cold. I'll make you something hot." She started to leave and then stopped. Mom and Lee helped her to the couch.

Mom said to Rosa, "Why don't I take you to the doctor?"

"*Cálmate*, Doña Julia," she said. "I'll stay here, please."

Mom left to make soup. Ruby jumped on Lee's lap. The cat comforted him in ways that I couldn't. I'd never been attracted to pet companionship, pet loyalty. Lee leaned back on my stomach. He told Rosa about a cold front coming from the north.

That night in bed, we watched the snow falling on the city. I squirmed under the blanket. We'd turned up the heat, but the room was still as cold as outside.

Lee said, "I talked to your father this morning."

I moved closer to him. "Why didn't you tell me?"

"I didn't want to bring him up with your mother around. I called him to go over some points of the contract. He thought maybe I'd want to work for Isla."

"I suggest you take your time and think about your next move."

"I respect your father's company. I was sure you'd want me to work for him."

What would Michael think of Lee's taking a job with Dad? What would Mom think? I said, "I want our lives to branch off from our work, not center on it so much."

He picked up a business magazine from the night table. He flipped through it and said, "Before I met you, all the girls I dated had one thing in common."

"What made you think of that?"

"Well, they were all extremely nice girls and they were all fine-looking. But they were all also gentle. Then you came along, and I thought to myself: She's a beauty because she's different—kind but tough."

"Tough?"

"Very. Remember how you told me you didn't trust anyone? That was showing your strength. Then one day—you'd cut class and we were in your dorm room—you told me, and you almost sounded mad about it, that you trusted me. But now I'm not sure you trust my judgment, Clarissa."

"What I don't trust is your consistency. Is it making you happy? You were ambitious when I met you; you're ambitious now. And it's the same kind of ambition. You must feel numb."

"I never viewed becoming successful as something exciting. There's monotony in success. I am consistent and I don't know how to be any other way. You'll have to show me."

"Don't think you have to take care of me so completely. That's the first lesson."

He looked as if he wanted to say something more. But what? I didn't try to guess. I preferred he tell me without my asking. He was a little like my father, I thought. Except for his desire to work, he implied his wishes; he expected others to discover them. I climbed on top of him. His body always felt hot. The sheets were tangled around my feet.

He kissed me. "I feel as if I'm kissing a doll," he said. And he gently pushed me off. "What's up?"

"I wonder if Rosa's dying."

In the middle of the night, the doorbell rang. Michael stood in the hall. He was in one of Dad's old sheepskin coats. He said, "Our dear mother locked me out. She chained the door." He smelled of snow. He was talking in a low voice. "I tried calling Mom's line, but she unplugged the phone. I could've knocked on the back door, but I'd wake Rosa." He collapsed on the couch and took off his coat and sweater. He rubbed his arms. "It's cold in here."

I got him a blanket and a pillow from my bedroom. A shadow slipped by me, Ruby heading for Lee.

I threw Michael the pillow and blanket. I said, "Have breakfast with us. This is kind of fun, like a sleepover."

He said, "Just like camp?"

•   •   •

In the morning, Michael and I walked to Mom's. Lee stayed home. He wanted to watch a football game and work. The chain was off the door when we got to Mom's. "She's up," Michael said. We let ourselves in and saw that Mom had gone back to her bedroom. I made breakfast for Rosa and Mom and thought I'd bring it to them in bed. I knocked on Mom's door.

"Where is your brother?" she said. She was tucking in the sheet. "I called Lee and he told me he was with you."

"You locked him out last night."

"Did I? I probably thought he was in bed. I've been so tired since Rosa's been sick. I'm just realizing all she does for us." She smoothed out the blanket. She looked at the cup of coffee on the tray. "You made me breakfast?"

I knocked before I entered Rosa's room. Her room was hot. She was sleeping on her stomach. I'd never seen her lie on her stomach. I said, "Time to get some food in you." She was still. I put down the tray. The vaporizer had no water in it and I unplugged the machine. I nudged Rosa's shoulder. I left the room to tell Michael that Rosa was dead. Then I went to tell Mom. She didn't say anything. I told her again. I had difficulty walking out of Mom's room.

Michael went back into Rosa's room with me. He said, "We have to change her." He folded his arms across his chest and then walked into her closet. He chose a black dress printed with large orange flowers. "Black," he said. "For a funeral." His eyes were bright and he looked to me as if he'd never blink again.

"Come downstairs with me," I said.

"You can help," he said and began undressing Rosa.

Mom opened the door. "Michael. Come with me. Now. Michael, you must leave Rosa alone." She grabbed him by the sleeve.

He removed her hand. He continued to unbutton Rosa's nightgown and said, "They rushed Rosa's father to the hospital, remember? And her mother threw away his work clothes and put him in a suit. Rosa told me she'd hope someone would do the same for her. So Mother, it's a matter of dignity." Michael picked up Rosa's brush. He cleaned out the hairs. His hands were trembling.

Mom was still; she watched Michael. She'd left the band off her caftan. She looked as if she were about to go to sleep. Michael threw the covers on the floor. He lifted Rosa's arms and slipped off her nightgown. One of her arms was bruised. I thought I should help him, but I felt dizzy. She was wearing one of Dad's old undershirts. The top of her chest was smooth. Michael left the undershirt on. I found myself helping Michael fit an arm through a sleeve. I smelled urine. He was buttoning Rosa's dress. I remembered the few times Rosa almost left the house with one or two buttons undone. I checked to see that Michael hadn't missed one.

When I got home, Edward was on the couch. Lee was sitting on the floor, facing him. Our sparse home, I thought, pointed to an emptiness in either Lee or me.

"What's the matter?" Edward said. He clanked down the cup of coffee. "Is someone going to tell me?"

I told them about Rosa. Lee guided me into our bedroom.

Edward said, "Rosa, your housekeeper? I'll make you some hot chocolate. Something hot . . ."

I held Lee. When Edward returned, I said, "I keep wondering whether she was surprised the moment she realized she was going to die. She was probably scared. . . ."

"You see, Lee," Edward said, "these things make you think about what matters."

"And what's that mean?" Lee said, looking away from his father.

"This isn't the time," Edward said. "Your wife's upset." He opened the window and leaned out. He was quiet until he sat back down. Then he said, "You think you have all the answers. Some fancy businessman comes up to you, you, a young boy, and this fancy man says to himself, Here's a good target. So he tells you he's got a deal you can't refuse, and you're with this man right away. . . ." He paused and stood. He puffed up a pillow for me to lean against. "Naturally, you get a lot of money for something that took over thirty years to build, but that's no matter. What matters is this: you have no idea what it's like to work for someone else. I do. Your own business gives you a place in the world. Tell me, son, what'll you do with all the money and time?"

"What we got, Pop—did you think the business was even worth that much?"

"What a terrible, unfair father I've been. Did I teach you to judge like that? If it were only a matter of money, I could have made quite a bit, some time ago. I had my offers. You think it was pride that prevented me from selling, or worse, stupidity? I'll tell you what it was," he said, pounding his chest. "Self-respect. And faith. And I still feel both. I'll take my fat share, and I say it's fat, and I'll live the rest of my life with your mother making whoopee with my share. I don't know you right now; I don't know where your feelings are." He shook his head. "Clarissa, I'm so sorry," he said. "God bless your Rosa." He walked out of the bedroom. The front door slammed.

Lee said, "The truth is, Clarissa, his business wasn't worth much: about one hundred and seventy thousand dollars, including whatever the equipment will bring." He shut the window. "I've been going to his warehouse, his customers, every day for the past five years, and then I come home and I stink and I have to get up and do it again and do it better than he did. He had me fooled. He told me he was making ends meet before he gave me the business. But he gave up on the business. Can't anyone see how much he had me fooled?"

"Why did you wait so long to tell me?"

"I was embarrassed for him." He left the bedroom.

Sleeping
Above
Home

"**J**ust, the problem is," Penn said, "you're under the power of your fucking house, you pathetic prince. I say we smoke the joint right here." Penn opened all the windows in the den and lit the joint. I was wrapping the curtain cord around my wrist, thinking: I'm really under the spell of one woman in this house. Mother had hired Faith Samson to take Rosa's place. That afternoon, they were both out. As Penn passed me the joint, I heard the front door open; and calmly, with my fingers, I snuffed the joint out and dropped it in my pocket. Mother walked in, with Faith behind her. That was when I got nervous, my hands shaking a little, not because I thought Mother would know what pot smelled like, but because of how Faith looked. She was now twenty-eight and I was seventeen. She had high cheekbones, a sharp nose and dark eyes, and a slow way of speaking.

Mother put down her purse and said to Faith, "It smells funny in here. What have you been using to clean?" She ran her finger along the table.

Penn stood to give her a kiss and said, "I smoked a clove cigarette. Sorry." He clutched his shirt pocket where the pack of cigarettes was. "You're looking spry, Missus Lyon."

Faith stood in the doorway, playing with the doorknob.

"I look the way I do now because I never smoked at your age," Mother said, and smiling, she pushed Penn away. Then she said to me, "I hope to tell that lawyer, any day now, I won't be needing his services anymore." She went into the bathroom and returned with a can of room freshener. As she was spraying, she said, "In time, your father will come to his senses. . . ." She turned to Penn. "Mister Lyon is going through a second childhood, studying bats as if he's working on a science experiment."

She'd been listening in on my phone calls, yet I didn't say anything because I didn't want to give her the chance to defend herself.

Faith asked Penn and me if we wanted anything. I said we didn't need anything, and Faith, wiping her hands on her hips, said to me, "Michael, maybe you know where I can take a class, maybe something to do with art." I liked the way she pronounced my name: My-kill.

"Yes, I've been talking to Faith about her schooling," Mother said. "She'd do well to take a class. But you must help her out."

"If you don't mind," Faith said, and she left, giving the doorknob one last twist.

Penn stared at me as if to say, You have all the luck, and then he went up to my room. As I was about to follow him, Mother, shaking up the can of room freshener, said, "Tell your sister I found the plants in her closet." She disappeared into the bathroom and shut the door.

Mother had given Cora three geranium plants when she'd come home a few weekends before. Cora hadn't wanted the plants; she'd said her roommate had too many plants as it was; and she shoved them in her closet before she hurried to catch her plane back to Chicago. I was supposed to throw them out, do something with them, before Mother found them, but I'd forgotten. I liked to blame my forgetfulness, not on my smoking pot, but on my acting: I was always memorizing lines. I wasn't talented, by any means—I was stiff, I was easily distracted—but my drama teacher, Ronald Eagle, seemed to believe I could get better, and he'd given me the part of Macbeth. The more I performed, especially when learning the part of Macbeth, the less I enjoyed acting. I was most content when reading plays alone. Still, I refused to give up, and my obstinacy kept me away from home almost every day: rehearsing.

Fingering the joint in my pocket, I told Mother as she came out of the bathroom, "I don't know why you keep buying Cora plants. She doesn't live here anymore."

"She most certainly does. She's at school, that's all. I thought she took the plants to school."

"She didn't want to hurt your feelings. Her roommate's allergic to flowers."

"Oh, of course," Mother said, "my feelings."

The next day, I rearranged my bedroom: I left all my books in the closet, but I took my football, baseball and notebooks off the shelves, and most of my clothes out of the drawers and closets, and packed them all into cardboard boxes. I threw away some old things—a stuffed blue dog, a collection of model airplanes, a box of corks, a bag of stolen hotel keys. Then I moved my couch under my loft, leaving a large space in the middle of the room. I figured I'd make myself a stage, and maybe, at the same time, I'd make Mother a little angry.

As I was closing up one of the boxes, Faith came in and glanced around my room. Her body was snug in a blue uniform. I noticed how short the hemline was. She said, "Are you moving out?"

No, I said. "I'm trying to simplify things."

"You have a big room," she said, "and a big house. In my country, my father and I shared our house with my uncle. We had a dock and ducks and a swing." She sat on the sofa and folded her hands on her lap. "One day, my cousin Joseph tied a rope around a duck so it couldn't use its wings, and he put the duck on the swing and made it fly into the street. I never—and I mean it—" she said, her hands moving excitedly, shell bracelets clicking together, "I never talked to Joseph again."

I said, "So how do you like New York?"

"I like being high above the streets. It makes me feel good."

I taped up a box of old clothes and asked her if she wanted any for her son.

"Yes. I'll get them to him. Thank you." But she was walking over to the wall, where she seemed more interested in the light switch, and I imagined taking her away to a beach somewhere where there were no rooms at all. She turned the light on, pushed the dimmer down, and the room went dark. She laughed and clapped her hands once and then said, no longer giggling, "What a funny thing."

I went to visit Clarissa and Lee one night after a long rehearsal. Lee was talking about beginning the training program at Isla. He wanted a company car and I remembered you'd promised him a Mercedes. He began joking about how little Spanish he knew. I thought your business possessed you, and now Lee had taken the place you reserved for me, which meant it would possess him, too. I didn't mind thinking that. I minded that I hadn't seen you in several months and that you called almost every night to talk to me about bats.

Clarissa poured me some wine.

Lee, rolling the television stand into the corner of the room, said to Clarissa, "Where should I put the fish tank? Here?" He was planning to build an aquarium, and Clarissa was against it.

Rolling the stand back to its place, she said, "The fish will die and you'll blame me." Then she folded up Lee's sketch for the aquarium and put it in a drawer. She was neat about placing it in the drawer, which made me think of Faith putting away a stack of my underwear in my drawer. Her hair smelling of cheap herbal shampoo. Well, well, she'd said, folding my things neatly, I didn't think you wore boxers.

"What do you say, Michael? We'll have a brigade of kissing fish," Lee said, "and a platoon of goldfish. I once met this man who told me he had several kinds of fish. One day, he lost his job and had no money and he ate the fish."

Clarissa said, "So if I run out of money and food, I have my fish."

"Faith's father won't eat fish," I said. "He believes they're ghosts." Stupid, bringing her up. Feel as if . . . sweating like a horse. Horses sweat where? Under the groin? Tucking in my shirt, I told Lee, "You'll bring your fish expertise to the stores. My father must be looking forward to that."

"Your father has given you so much," he said. "Why do you sound as if you resent him?"

One late night in March, after Mother had gone to sleep, my bedroom door opened. It was Faith and she said, "Do you want me here?"

I told her yes. As she climbed into my bed, she told me, "You should go after what you want."

Faith stayed with me until about five in the morning. Then, dressing, she said, "Should we do this again?"

"I think we have to."

"We have to? Aren't you something! We have to be careful, is what. Don't tell your friend Penn about us. Don't tell anyone. I need this job: I want to save money and buy things. I'll get something for my son. Something for my father. And a few things for me."

Faith was sprawled on the floor, a blanket under her. We'd been lovers for almost two months. I was in her room; it was close to three in the morning. Faith said, turning onto her back and staring at the ceiling, "Adam's father is somewhere in this city. His name's Peque. No one thought I knew who the father was, but I knew. Adam looks like him. I've never told anyone this, but Peque would've married me if I'd told him about the baby. But I said to myself, I deserve better."

"Did you come here to find him?" I said, surprised to feel jealous.

"Peque?" She laughed.

The way she said his name made me feel brave: I pictured us both in front of the Lincoln Center fountain kissing in daylight and I said, "Let's go out for lunch next week."

After a while, she told me that might be nice. Then she moved closer to me, her hair falling into her face, and she whispered, "I was thinking about my mother. Sometimes my mother hated herself for marrying a black man, and sometimes she'd look at me and say, 'Too bad I'm not black.' "

She kissed me and I stopped her. "Why'd she say that?"

"She was only wishing for one more thing to have in common with him. I could say something like that about you: Too bad I'm not rich." She took my hand, studied my fingers, straightened my pinkie, and bit off my nail. "Your nail," she said. "I'll keep this. Your come, or your spit would be nice, too, but this will last longest."

"But you don't work," Faith was telling me another day, her hands on her waist. She had on a slip. "How do you buy yourself things? How do you buy me things?"

That morning, I'd told Penn about my affair and then asked him to help me pick out a belt for Faith; I admired her small waist.

"I get an allowance. Twenty dollars a week," I said. I lay on her bed, next to a piece of paper. On it, she'd drawn a plus sign and a minus sign. With my help, she'd found a design class and had been talking about her assignment—to illustrate tension—for the past half hour.

"What's the twenty dollars for?" She was buckling the belt on top of her slip.

"For being a son. That's a responsibility these days, in families like mine."

"You're making fun of me." She then pointed to the paper and said, "Tension. Now I think I'll hand in a Polaroid of you and me before sex. . . . Yes, you were too rough last night; you hurt me."

I wanted to make up for hurting her, so I started taking off my clothes, taking off hers, though she was not helping at all. Then I heard the door downstairs slam and Mother calling my name. I grabbed my clothes, ran to my room and got in the shower.

Mother came into my bathroom, and I turned off the water, reached for a towel and yelled, "What do you want?"

"Did your father call?"

"No. Please let me shower."

"He's going to call soon. Don't you think?" She started to close my bathroom door and then said, "I have my pride, you know. I can't be the one to offer solutions. I didn't leave him. Don't you think I have my pride?"

Lennox, played by Arlo, sat on the edge of the stage, twirling Pauline's long blond braid around his arm. It was the dress rehearsal, and I sat on the other side of Pauline, who was Lady Macbeth. I said to her, "Where's Matt?"

She whispered, "He says he's tired of Eagle and his antics. He may not show up. I told him he better not ruin it for the rest of us." She sighed and said, "You're not happy with the play. I saw you in *The Tempest*. You were much more relaxed then."

"'I keep thinking Macbeth should just kill himself."

She said, "That's a weird thought."

I said I was just kidding. Then I said, "I'm sorry I don't do justice to your Lady."

The dress rehearsal was getting off to a slow start, and I kicked my heels against the stage, wondering if Matt, who was Banquo, would show. Ronald Eagle was making us do three dress rehearsals and we all had finals. He sat in the sixth row, reading a stack of papers. Arlo stretched, stood and began to tap-dance.

"He's in a foul mood," Pauline said of Eagle.

I said, tired from having stayed up all night with Faith, "We're all too worked up," and Arlo tap-danced again.

Matt walked in and said to me, "This production is a joke."

We were about to begin, and Ronald Eagle asked everyone to quiet down, as the backstage rustling and laughter filtered through the dropped curtain. A collection of voices, one voice maybe one day becoming famous. Who'd be in films? Who'd do cereal commercials? Who'd give up?

After the rehearsal, during which I forgot two lines, Ronald Eagle followed me into the street. He said, "You take the subway home, don't you? Mind if I ride with you?" We went down the steps of the Eighty-sixth Street station and he said, "What do you think of Macbeth?"

The train arrived and we hurried on and found two seats. I said, "I'm not sure," and thought of Faith telling me about her son having cut off part of his finger while playing with a machete at a friend's house. I said to Ronald Eagle, "I like Macbeth best at the start of the play, when he's satisfied with things." I didn't say the obvious: with the help of Lady Macbeth, Macbeth becomes ambitious and rapidly unhappy. "Art thou afeard to be the same in thine own act and valor as thou art in desire?" Pauline would say to me. And I thought: Macbeth is trapped by Lady Macbeth; I'm trapped by Faith's smell and touch.

Ronald Eagle smoothed back his hair, as he liked to do before a brief lecture, and he said, "Chebutykin in *Three Sisters* is my favorite character. 'Perhaps I'm not even a human being, perhaps I only pretend to have arms and legs and a head, perhaps I don't even exist at all, and only imagine I walk about and eat and sleep. . . .' I only pretend to have arms. . . ." He glanced at me and laughed. "Michael, your Macbeth only *pretends* to be a killer. I don't feel he *is* one. He moves and speaks like a dejected teenager. We don't want people thinking we can't act beyond our years, do we?"

One school morning, Faith climbed into my bed. Her nightgown felt cool, and she told me, "Shhh, we have to be quiet."

I opened my eyes. "My mother's probably up." I rolled onto a copy of *Macbeth* I'd fallen asleep reading.

Faith threw the book off the bed. "Your mother's sleeping. I wanted to wake up next to you."

I said, "I want what you do." I fell back asleep and dreamed of Faith lying beside me. She must have slept, too. When Mother knocked, I thought I was still dreaming, but Faith quickly got up and out of bed. She shook me and whispered, "Tell her you'll be ready in a minute."

But Mother had already entered the hall of my bedroom, telling me I was going to be late, and she saw Faith. Turning away, Mother said, "What loyalty you both show me." Then she went up to Faith and took her by the shoulders and pushed her out of the room. I followed them. Mother was pushing Faith down the hall, down the stairs. They were going out the apartment's front door.

I shouted, "Mother, ask *me* what this is about."

But Mother was already out in the hall, pushing the elevator button. She stared at me, and then at Faith, and she said, "I shall ask you no such thing."

Faith said to her, "I'll leave, Missus Lyon, but if I could just change . . ." Then she began whispering to herself as she rubbed one of her shoulders, where Mother's palm had left an imprint.

The doors of the elevator opened. Mother pointed to the elevator and said, "Get out of my home, Faith Samson, out this minute."

The elevator man, who'd told me twice he was a born-again Christian, peered out at us, and I told him he could go. Then I noticed someone else in the elevator, the Nigerian ambassador, a tall, quiet diplomat to whom Cora had once spoken, a diplomat acting oblivious to a dark-skinned woman in a nightgown and a fair-skinned woman in a robe. Mother also noticed him and let go of Faith's arm.

"We're staying," I said to the elevator man.

He said, as the door began to close, "God bless you and keep you."

Mother, in the kitchen, was doing Faith's morning chores. I was with Faith in her bedroom, watching her pack. She said, "I miss my son."

I didn't believe her. Whenever she spoke of Adam, she spoke only of his father, Peque.

"I shouldn't have come to you," Faith said and began to look for something.

I thought: I've betrayed Mother; I've betrayed Faith.

Faith came over to me and touched my chin. "You're comfortable with yourself; you're strong—yes, your strength is your greatest appeal."

"My appeal."

"These days, my strength comes from having sex with you and from hoping to see you again. Your strength comes from somewhere else that has nothing to do with me. I envy you. You have purpose. I have luck: here you were, right next door to me."

I held her.

"We were all over this house," she said softly, "and now everything here makes me feel low."

I'd made her feel that way. I stopped hugging her.

After Faith left, I went across town to stay at Penn's for a few days. I stopped in a coffee shop and ordered coffee, wanting to think of something besides Faith. . . . I thought of *Macbeth*. The last play of the Shakespeare Festival. And I hadn't done well with it. Muscular memory—a phrase of Stanislavski's: I hadn't moved like a king; I'd moved like a lover sneaking into Faith's bed. But, I told myself, if I'd allowed myself to feel as tormented as Macbeth had, I'd never allow the torment to stop. Of course, that was why I'd failed.

That evening, Penn and I played chess. We'd been on the same game for an hour, and every time I was about to lose a man, Penn warned me to make another move.

He said, "The other day, I found out I got into Bennington College, but let's face it: school's too much like a cage. I'm leaving town and sailing for the Grenadines. With Captain Thomas Neville Thorn. I call him TNT. I'll be free and I'll be making good money. And here's the best part: I don't know when I'm coming back."

"I guess that's the right thing for you to do." And I envied him and wondered if I could also get a job as a sailor.

He took my knight and said, "How's your woman?"

"She left."

"Here's a secret, Just. Never let a woman knock you off your feet. Terrible way to be, without your feet. Have you heard of these terrorists in Peru who cut off their victims' feet? Then they sew them on backward. That way the dead can't follow them."

"Aren't you tired of putting on your invincibility act?"

I waited for his response and thought he seemed tired or even older, with his torn jeans and dirty fingernails and messy hair. Without looking away from the board, he smiled and said it was my turn, and I felt that his banter was lately revealing a cynicism he'd have preferred to keep hidden from me. We played the rest of the game in silence, as if appreciative of each other's disappointments.

The next day, Mother called Penn's house and asked me to come home. I didn't want to, not right away, so I walked up First Avenue to Ninety-sixth Street and then I walked home.

Mother was waiting for me in the foyer. She kissed me when I came in and she said, "I was so angry with you and Faith. I got such a scare. I just can't watch you end up like your father."

"What does Dad have to do with this?"

"Just be careful what you do, please. . . . I'll run myself a bath and we'll have some—" She pulled me to her and she held me. "Stay like that. Aren't we a sad pair?"

I pulled away and walked into the den, where the cuckoo bird was just slipping into the clock. Mother followed. I said, "You don't want me to 'end up' like my father? What does that mean?"

"I meant me, Michael, concerning me." She hugged herself. "Your father made the wrong choice. Isn't that what he's trying to tell me? And my god, just look what we've become."

Positioning the Animals

Father was taking me to the caves, on a rocky trail through the woods. He moved with remarkable stealth, as if he'd been on the trails of Bat Island countless times before. Soon he bent down to sift through the leaves, twigs and dirt. Confidently, he said, "What I'm looking for, Cora, is discarded pieces of prey. The short-tailed fruit bat eats only moths, grasshoppers and beetles. They suck out the fluids and the tissues—the protein, that is—and they get rid of everything else."

"Then why are they called fruit bats?"

Holding his magnifying glass over his stomach, he glanced up as if he expected a particular bat to be flying above him. "Well, they eat fruit, too. Why, of course they do: they fly over a banquet every night, but they only take the fruit that's too ripe for us. And they scatter the seeds all over the forest to keep it rich, to keep it fertile with possibilities."

"Dad, you're charmed." He was enthralled: a Naive Explorer. I delighted in being alone with him on Bat Island; I was not looking forward to Clarissa, Lee and Michael's arriving in a few days. I took the magnifying glass from his hand and held it up to the stars. "So where are these fruit bats?"

"*Paciencia,*" he said. "They'll be heading for their night roosts soon. . . . They'll go home early tonight. The moon's full." He beamed his flashlight on a large leaf where a bat had nibbled along the main vein: the leaf had collapsed to form a tent. Then he described how the bat hung, camouflaged, ceremonious, under the tent to eat. He whispered, "Do you see the beauty in them? How the light dictates their habits?"

"You're more than charmed. You want to fly." I laughed. "So what other kinds of bats? Vampires?"

"Must be a few Mexican bulldogs. I wonder: do they prey on frogs? They echolocate—that's their form of sonar—"

"I know what echolocation is."

"All right," he said. Had I embarrassed him? No—he pushed on: "Bats. Divine animals. Next time, I'll remember the bat detector." He pointed toward a clearing in the woods, through which we could see a black ribbon of beating wings.

What was he trying to tell me? What was this about divine mammals?

Slinging his arm around my shoulder, he said, "I knew you'd feel better once you stayed with me. Now finish up school. Look after yourself."

How did he know I hadn't? I was still on forty milligrams of cortisone, tapering slowly. I knew that the drug might alter my mood; at school, I'd surely felt a little depressed. I'd found the classrooms cold and confining. So I drove around Michigan, Wisconsin and Indiana with a pack of friends. We did whatever drug we wanted—Quaaludes and black beauties, our favorites—and I ended up, feverish and pouting, in a hospital bed. (As I put on the hospital gown, I thought: At least I know why I'm sick this time—I haven't looked after myself.)

"Here we go," Father said and lifted in his palm a star-like twig. "This was once a cricket."

"Now it's a twig."

"You're not looking at it," he said. He was gentle, persuading, as he picked up a larger twig. "This is a twig."

The next morning, I walked to town. I was barefoot and careful to step over dried squashed frogs. I was toughening myself. Why not begin with calluses on the soles? But soon enough, I stepped on a thorn. My foot was hot and throbbing.

I sat on a bench in front of Martha Megran's general store and scraped at the thorn in my heel. A Help Wanted sign was posted in the window, next to a handwritten sign: *10% off Coca-Cola.* A man and woman were leaving the store, on their way to the hotel. The man was portly. He wore white Bermuda shorts, a blue shirt and loafers with white socks. He was arguing with the woman, no doubt his wife. She was chubby. She wore a long yellow skirt with a flowered blouse and flat red shoes. What was their routine? I wondered, as he pointed to his polished shoes. Did he criticize her? And did she defend herself? Did he then ridicule her even more? They lingered near the stone wall that protected the hotel from the wind, the man now pointing to the woman's scuffed-up shoes. I was trying to be curious . . . frankly, I was trying to appreciate people again. In September, I'd turn twenty. My prejudices had become too cunning and odious. On the plane down, I'd sat next to a man wearing a red suit. His sneakers were the high-top kind, with blue stripes. He smelled like rotting wood. I felt indignant; I almost took another seat at the back of the plane. I detested how his odor, that is, any odor, offended me; I detested how particular I was about cleanliness and appearance.

I told myself I was going to be comfortable on this island. Few people lived here. I knew the people well enough, though no one—and I gave thanks for this—knew how sick I'd been. Penn knew, I thought; Penn didn't mind. He'd been a friend when I'd been both ill and well. Was that why I thought of him constantly? He'd written me from every island he'd sailed to in the Caribbean. While reading his letters, I imagined him on a roof, holding a bottle of beer from Malta. I wanted to be loyal to him, but I compromised my loyalty and then became enraged with myself. I hadn't been faithful: I'd gone out with an engineering student, whose smile reminded me of Penn's; I'd gone out with a chef, who told me he was falling in love with me. I tactfully ended both "situations" by saying, "I've been miraculously reconciled with an old love."

Thirsty, I went into the coffee shop and sat at a table under a palm tree in the garden. Soon Mitchell Willet strolled in. His feet were burned, red skin crisscrossed by leather thongs, and his short-sleeve white shirt was tucked tightly into his shorts. I asked him to join me.

"Yes, a good cup of coffee keeps me fit," he said. He started to fiddle with his watch. It looked like the kind with an alarm and a calculator. He then took the watch off and put it on the table. He ordered two cappuccinos. "You're staying here this summer, Cora? I am, too. Here I'm free of bankers, stockbrokers and lawyers. I only have to make peace with myself. I used to travel all the time. We went to Chile, Australia, Africa . . . but I never got to India. Sara, my wife, didn't care to go to India."

He never talked about his wife for long, as if he wanted to keep her memory to himself. I played with his watch; I pressed a tiny button. Something beeped.

"Shark alarm," Willet told me. "When you're diving with a buddy, that'll warn him about a shark. I'd like you to keep the watch."

I picked up the watch and examined the buttons. I thanked him many times. He was trying to be friendly. Maybe we had much more in common than I saw. Maybe he felt as repelled by people as I did. I said, "Why don't you let anyone go in the caves?"

"It's dangerous: I once knew a fellow who caught pneumonia. And besides, too much cave snooping scares off the bats. Even if you think you know the caves, you can disturb the environment without realizing it, and the smallest disturbance may turn into a disaster."

"Are there any vampires here?"

"They're only in Central and South America," he said. "Which causes trouble for other bats. The farmers are always killing colonies of non-vampires along with the vampires. They use fire and napalm."

"That's what everyone's good at: tampering."

"Exactly! And what they choose to tamper with! Vampires are terribly maligned creatures; in fact, less than one percent carry rabies. They're ingenious. They have cheek teeth that scissor away any fur or feathers; and their saliva has an anticoagulant."

"But do they really bite people?"

"Only if they're very hungry and can't find a docile cow or dog. And after they feed, vampires urinate to rid their blood of anything that weighs them down."

"Blood's heavy as it is," I said, assertive. I'd been anemic; I knew the properties of blood. "We bat-watch. My father's very careful."

Willet drank some of his cappuccino. Then, looking in the cup, he said, "Your father is an invisible man when he's here, which is odd. In Puerto Rico, he socializes as if he can't live without it."

"So . . . maybe my father's feeling dead," I said lightly.

"How could that be? Your father's a man of good fortune: he has his children. And how is your mother?"

After coffee, Willet helped me pick out a cedar bat house for Father. He said to me, "Perhaps you and your father would like to join me for dinner one evening."

I told him we would. Then I left him, to ask for the job at the general store. Martha Megran, a large woman with a weathered face, had wrinkles around her mouth that gave her the appearance of smiling all the time. She demurely tipped her yellow hat and said, "You could be my stock girl. I could use you, honey."

When I got home, Father was on the terrace, snipping away at wire mesh, measuring screens to batproof the house. He was proud of my new job. "Just like your father," he bellowed.

"Mitchell Willet invited us over for dinner one night," I said.

Father flattened some leftover mesh into what looked like a wing, which he flapped once or twice. His silence was deadening, I thought, as I slipped the watch into my pocket.

Cautious, I said, "Why don't you like him?"

He stopped playing with the mesh. "I don't like to be disapproving, but I don't care for his style. A business associate of mine told me Mitchell Willet broke a very significant contract with him, which was of great embarrassment to my friend. Someone else told me . . . What's the difference? For Christ sakes, Cora, it's a question of loyalty and . . ." He paused to lift his forefinger. ". . . and courtesy. If a man disregards his own honor, how can he value another man's?"

I asked myself: Why not?

Holding the razor firmly, I cut open the cardboard box of peeled Italian tomatoes. It was my fourth day at work. Clarissa, Lee and Michael had flown in that morning. I held the price gun firmly and fixed a label on each can. I was in the stockroom. There were many unopened boxes stacked against the walls. Martha helped me load the opened box of tomatoes onto a trolley, which I wheeled out into the store. She said, "If Terrence comes in, tell him dinner's at eight. I'm hurrying to the post office."

I tidied up. It started to rain, and I stood at the window, looking at the downpour. I saw Father, and then Lee, running toward the store, trying to avoid the small puddles already in the streets. They came inside the store. Out of breath, they rested at the check-out counter. Lee, wiping water from his face with his hand, said, "Nice shop you got here."

Father checked to see how damp his cigar had become in his shirt pocket. "Give me a grand tour," he said.

I took the two of them into the stockroom, where water was leaking through a corner of the ceiling and falling into a rusty tin that Martha had left on the floor.

"What markups!" Father said as he picked up a can of juice. "We sell this for twenty-nine cents." He opened a closet, brought out an old ladder and put all his pressure on one rung. "Your ladder isn't safe. You need to keep your props in excellent shape."

I heard someone outside. Frightened it was Martha, I told Lee and Father to please be polite. But it was only Terrence, rudely shuffling his cumbersome feet. I gave him Martha's message.

"Wonderful! I look forward to a home-cooked meal," he said. "How are you, Mister Lyon?"

"Everyone's healthy, Mister Huston, thank you."

Lee nodded his head in a stiff greeting. He left the store. He'd told me he had little to say to a man like Terrence, someone who fabricated aspects of himself.

Terrence tapped a few boxes of sugar on the shelf. He said to me, "If you're part of Martha's establishment, you should know I need my sugar."

I worried that he'd knock the lovely row of sugar down, which would, like falling dominoes, hit the even lovelier row of brown sugar and cinnamon.

"Martha gives me a box of sugar every week," he said. "Without my sugar, I feel too wired." He chose a box and tucked it under his arm. "Martha's gift. Tell her I was here."

"Peculiar man," Father said after Terrence left. "Peculiar way to run a business."

Soon Martha walked in, whistling one of my favorite calypso tunes, "Yellow Bird." She was holding two packages. "Come in the back," she said to Father. "Damn rain. You can bet there'll be no morning deliveries from the Virgin Islands tomorrow."

"Terrence took some sugar," I told her as I straightened a stack of empty boxes in the stockroom.

Father added, "Very gracious of you to give him free orders."

Martha ripped the paper off one package. "He's my blood, so to speak. Besides, I don't have thousands of stockbrokers to answer to, as you do, and so I give as freely as I wish." She held out a flat brown box to Father. She whispered, "You're a true connoisseur; you'll appreciate these." The cigar box was nailed shut. She opened it and revealed the treasure: Cuban cigars, Monte Cristo.

"You must know the right people," Father said, immensely pleased.

Clarissa stepped onto the terrace, where I sat eating some cookies Father had half baked. Michael was near me, reading. Lee pointed out a constellation to Clarissa. He made up a name, the Running Amazon. My sister placed her hand on Lee's lower back.

Lee said, "I finished building my fish tank. Clarissa gave me some beautiful freshwater fish. One's already died. But a fish has to die to christen the tank."

"Bat at northwest, I think," Michael said and looked toward the cliff as Father came to join us.

I was no longer frightened of the true vampire, the *Desmodus rotundus,* Father had called it. Nor would I tremble at the thought of the *Vampyrodes caraccioli,* a misnomer, a non-vampire bat, a tailless creature. Neither one had fangs.

"I don't like those bats," Clarissa said. Always the one to spot a jewel, she looked at my watch. "Where'd you get that? It looks like a man's watch."

"Mitchell Willet gave it to me. If you knew anything about watches, my dear, you would know this is a diving watch."

Father sat down at the end of my lounge chair. "Mister Willet wishes he had children like you," he said. He lit his cigar with one swift motion. "Listen, it's time we talk about your mother. It's only fair you know what's going on. She, as you know, doesn't want to give me a divorce, which makes no sense. . . ." He sucked on the cigar. "We haven't even had normal relations in who knows how long."

Lee excused himself to look over a report.

Michael kept his head down. He said, "Relations?"

Father, cocooned in the rewards of his cigar and the company of his children, said, "Michael, your mother has become a different woman because of me. She's lost herself by devoting herself to me. But maybe I'm responsible for the way we've turned out. That's why I left." He fumbled in his pocket for the cigar cutter and said when he found it, "This is sixty years old."

Michael asked, "May I try your cigar?"

Father relit the cigar. He quickly handed it to Michael, with a grin that implied: This tobacco is the supreme indulgence.

"What's it feel like to be a father who smokes a cigar and tells his kids how it is?" Michael said.

"Give it back," Father said. He took the cigar and promptly snapped it in two. He squared off the tattered ends and gave one half to Michael, saying. "A father would have one of his own."

Michael tossed the half cigar. He sauntered away.

"I'm sorry I've made your brother dislike me so much," Father

said to me and Clarissa. "But there are things you should know,
so you can learn. I think of all the times—"
    I said, furiously ripping apart a small coconut, "Dad—"
    "Let me finish, Cora."
    "What's with you?" I heard myself say. "Why do you think we
have to know every little truth?"
    He was quiet.
    I wasn't. "Every little truth about every little bat . . ."

I ran to town and then walked to the caves. I hoped everyone
was tucked, warm and tense, in bed. Father, I thought, was too
demanding of all of us; as for me, he wanted me back in school.
But I fancied staying in the city, close to all my doctors. My fear
was detestable—I knew that—as was my desire to live close to
Mother, who was so used to being my nurse. I thought: If I could
only be like Clarissa, dodging my own solitude. Or if only Penn
. . . I remembered Penn had said: You don't want a boyfriend.
You're all locked up. He might as well have said: You don't want
normal relations.
    I swung my flashlight freely, hit my hip a few times. The
insects and frogs were too loud. Each creature sang to its own
rhythm. Turning the flashlight off, I walked through the pale
glow of the evening. I stepped on something warm and wet.
Maybe Terrence's car had rolled over a frog on his way home
from Martha's. I pictured the frog's twisted skin and tissue, so
much like the uneven topography of the island. Hurrying over
the bridge, I thought: If the bats have left for their hunt, it'll be
safe to go into the caves.
    I stood at the mouth of a cave. The cave opened into a
dome-like den at the bottom of a slope. I heard trickling water
and felt the cold air inside. Oh, but I was an Informed Explorer.
I turned the flashlight on. The guano—it looked like black
paint—was splattered all over the cave walls. I crept in farther
and noticed an opening in the ceiling as large as a manhole,
through which the stars were shining. A few bats flew by me. A
stream flowed deeper into the cave and then into smaller caverns. Water dripped steadily, rhythmically, from stalactites.

"You're brave, like me," I heard. His voice sounded hoarse. He sat near a column, a stalagmite joined to a stalactite. He turned his flashlight on.

I was scared, as if he weren't my father at all. I asked him what he was doing there.

"I was thinking about what you said."

I was embarrassed I'd babbled. Babbling idiots found no favor with me.

He said, "I ask too much of you. And of Michael. And of Clarissa. And maybe even of Lee." He touched the column. "It's beautiful by day in here, but it's better for the bats if you visit by night. Come, I'll show you." He headed toward the caverns in the back of the den and pointed his flashlight on the ceiling. Hundreds of bats were fluttering in a small hole. Hundreds of insects covered the ground, making it appear to move. The stench of guano was strong.

Father turned on the bat detector, a small gray plastic box with a tiny megaphone. What strange calls these bats had: a hum that loudened and sometimes softened.

"When they're feeding, the buzzes speed up," Father said, boyishly tilting the bat detector. "They can catch one hundred and fifty mosquitoes within fifteen minutes."

"Mitchell Willet says you can get pneumonia in these caves."

"We're okay; plenty of air from that hole over there," he said and crossed the stream to leave the cave.

Outside, I retreated to a rock, the cut on my heel having reopened. I rubbed a colony of ants into the ground with my foot. The ants tickled a raw piece of my skin.

"What's that noise?" I said when Father came over to me, after washing his hands in the ocean.

"A boat . . . Prowling teenagers, probably."

Then I heard boys shouting. What jubilant cries! as if they were playing war. Soon the boat whirred away. Father took a cigar from his shirt pocket and began to peel off one of its leaves. He said, "Exceptionally made." He was still unraveling the cigar. "Exceptionally made."

With Speed

Lee was in San Juan. He'd started the training program at Isla. He called me almost every night. I didn't miss him. Instead, I was looking at him as if we'd just become friends. He was dedicated to his work. I didn't find that admirable anymore. I asked myself who he'd be if he lost his job.

I had the apartment to myself; I had time to myself. Suddenly I was examining my looks. My hair seemed too dark; I had it highlighted. Then I went to the Philharmonic to hear *The Rite of Spring* and the next night to Carnegie Hall to hear Juilliard student recitals. Some of the students looked too young and eager to please. One day, I went to the Steinway store and pretended I wanted to buy a piano. I felt content playing the pianos in the store, even purposeful.

After work, I had drinks with people from the office. They drank a lot and became cynical about their jobs. I didn't drink a lot. But I looked at other men in the restaurant. I wondered if I'd be more at ease with another man. Or if another man would be more at ease with me. I thought if only I could fall in love with another man, I'd have a reason to leave. The problem so far seemed to be that I had no good reason for feeling discontent. Several times, I invited Cora over for dinner. She was on a leave of absence from school and was staying with Mom. She told me I'd picked up Mom's habit of closing my eyes when I was annoyed. Once, when I went to Mom's for dinner, Mom told me, "You look as if you're wasting away. Darling, without Lee keeping you on your toes, you're half a person."

One weekend morning, not quite on my toes, I stood in front of the full-length mirror in our bedroom. My period was late. I didn't want to be a mother. I was twenty-four, dependent on a man I disliked much of the time. I'd never counted on feeling dependent on anyone. And I thought that was a good reason to leave Lee. Yet I was not much better off when he left me alone. "So, Missus Berryman," I said aloud, "why blame him for your unhappiness?" I stared at myself for almost half an hour. Then I put on a pair of Lee's jeans and one of his sweaters. I stared at myself some more. I put a towel over the mirror and stood in the darkness.

Lee and I had planned on my taking a week's vacation in Puerto Rico. I left the next day, feeling unprepared for the trip.

I sunbathed in our backyard in Santa María. Lee was at work. I noticed how much prettier, like a small plot of forest, the yard looked under Dad's hand or lack of handling. I was reading the *San Juan Star*, an article about a bomb scare. A few days earlier, on March 12, the Independentistas had bombed three post offices and a navy recruiting office. There was an interview with Rubén Berríos. He was a graduate of Yale Law School and the head of the Independence Party. He said he had no ties with the terrorists. There was another interview, with Governor Romero Barceló of the New Progressive Party, the party for statehood. Barceló talked about the unfairness of the commonwealth status: the States used almost all the funds for social services, even though Carter promised to get Puerto Rico at least fifteen million

a year for its social services. . . . Isla was fighting to stay open Sundays. The 1902 Closing Law said businesses had to be closed Sunday. The courts were temporarily forbidding the stores to stay open every day. . . . A car accident had killed a teenager. . . . Hector Gútierrez of Guaynabo married Adelaida Santiago of Vega Baja. Teresa Alonso of Cataño had a baby boy. . . . Charles Wilson's oil company was folding. . . . A new advertising campaign for a suntan lotion, Tropidream, had just come out. It featured Miss Puerto Rico.

I thought of a focus group I'd joined in Kansas City for a new toy campaign. In a small room, I'd watched and listened to a dozen housewives through a two-way mirror. My agency was paying each of them two hundred dollars. They were asked to talk about how well a slogan described a toy ball. The ball was transparent, with trees, lakes, stick figures and dogs floating inside. We were marketing the ball as a miniature globe for two-year-olds. The line—"Put a world in your child's hands"—bothered some women. One woman said it sounded as if one were spoiling one's child. Another woman said her boy was scared of dogs. Another held up the ball and said, "The world's not so playful." She said it again, more harshly. She must have been in her fifties. She wore a light blue dress and her hair was curled. The account executive said to the man who had assembled the group, "Let's get rid of that one, right away." After she was asked to leave, I wondered what she'd been thinking. Maybe she thought she'd made an easy two hundred dollars. And maybe she thought that one day she'd like to be working in a position where she could dismiss someone on the spot.

I folded up the newspaper. I strolled back to the house. I wanted to shower and take a pregnancy test. I went into the bathroom and waited for the test to show me something. The strip of paper turned blue; that meant positive. I felt as if Lee had betrayed me. I threw water on my face.

Four friends of Dad's—Martin, Taco (Leonardo, his real name), Henry and Eddie—arrived. Henry came on his Pasofino. He lived a few blocks away and had a stable. Taco and Eddie drove

in from San Juan, Martin from Old San Juan. Eddie rolled two
cigarettes with blue rolling paper as soon as he walked in. The
smoke bothered Martin. The men liked to play poker to Leonard
Bernstein. They'd listen to *On the Town* and *West Side Story*.
Taco and Henry had a contest going: who could do more card
tricks? Dad brought in two bottles of Château Larose-Trintaudon
and a bottle of Blanc-de-Blanc. Eddie got himself a beer from the
refrigerator. Henry asked Dad for a glass of white wine, but Dad
went to put Bernstein on. Martin began shuffling the cards. I
smiled at them all. I liked how intoxicated they were by the
game.

I asked Lee to go for a walk. The Pasofino stood in our garage
gnawing carrots, which Henry had left on the floor. I pointed out
to Lee the homes of old neighbors. He talked about learning
Spanish. Then he said, "Will you come to the store tomorrow?"

I said I would.

He said, "So much is happening: this job, all this deciding
whether or not we should move. It may be smart to start asking
your father about the agencies down here."

"I'm pregnant."

He put his arm around me. He kissed my cheek.

I was nervous. "You told me you wanted a baby soon," I said.
"Remember? I know I told you it was too early. When was I
careless?"

"You said you wanted a family."

"I say a lot of things I don't mean. Why don't you know that?"

"On the way to work, your father told me, Clarissa's scared of
having a family. I said, That's one thing she's not scared of."

It was almost eleven. All of Dad's friends had left but Martin.
Smoke was settling on the wineglasses, salad plates, turkey skins.
Someone had spilled wine on the tablecloth.

Dad rubbed his chest and stifled a yawn. He said, "The priests
are hoping they can revive this Closing Law. But it's archaic
already."

"What this law is," Martin said, "is the Church pulling its
weight: pulling on people's fears."

Lee said, "The customers will be on our side."

"Well, I'll be going to work Sundays," Dad said. "I'll learn all about the Puerto Rican constitution." He turned to Lee. "Supermarkets . . . Martin's in the circus. That's what I call a reliable business." He went to fetch another bottle of wine. When he came back, he said, "Here's a little treat: a Saint-Émilion from 1959. A Cheval Blanc. Jerry Case, that wine importer from Texas, gave me this."

Martin said to Lee, "I'm sending my son to Bordeaux to pick the grapes. He thinks he's going to have fun. Fun! He has no idea the hard work he's in for!" Martin had dark, hollow-looking eyes. I couldn't tell where his pupil met his iris. His eyes bothered me. I glanced at Lee's eyes. They were clear. They seemed innocent, as if they'd never seen anger or filth. Even when he worked late, Lee's eyes were clear.

Dad was decanting the wine. He said, "You want to go pick grapes, Lee?"

Lee brushed crumbs into his hand and then into the ashtray. "I'd rather go to the circus. When's it coming?"

"It's here every spring," Martin said. "Summer's too hot for the animals. Listen to this act: I've got a woman who rides two lions at a time. On their noses. And she's naked."

"Naked, my foot," Dad said. He poured the wine.

I said, "I remember going to your circus. You had the most wonderful clown family. A baby clown, a dog clown, a wife with blue hair. And the father clown played a beautiful organ that I always wanted to play."

"A calliope, my dear. Yes, that one was from Barnum and Bailey," Martin said. "Carlos was a damn good clown, too. Good clowns are tough to come by: only a few have a true spirit."

Dad held up his wineglass. He said, "To my oldest daughter and my fellow worker. Martin, Lee's at the Santa María store now."

"Welcome to our humble island," Martin said. "Where will you live?" He swished the wine back and forth in the glass. "My lord, look at the legs on this wine!"

Dad smiled. Then he said, "Lee doesn't have to move. He'll just have to travel a bit." He sipped the wine.

Martin sipped his. He said, "Vinegar."

I tried the wine. It tasted a little tart but smooth. I let it linger in my mouth, as Dad had taught me.

Dad rotated the decanter. "The cork must have leaked," he said. He put his hand on Martin's shoulder and started laughing. "Oh, well, the cork was damp, you know. So much for Jerry Case. But I'd never have the heart to tell him."

"What about recorking?" Lee said. "You think that could've helped?"

Dad told him that recorking was a tricky business.

I tasted the wine again. I said, "I think it's fine."

Dad said, "Sweetheart, you can't drink this."

"I like it." With my second glass the wine softened. The bouquet opened up to me. Sediment lined the bottom of the glass. We talked some more about the Closing Law. And I felt drunk when I said, "Families are like circuses. But family members are never, as you say, Martin, clowns with *true* spirits. What I mean is this: their spirit comes from something far from joy."

"What's that?" Dad asked. He poured some cognac.

"But there are always nets in families," I continued. I was pleased with myself, even though I could see I was making Lee uncomfortable. "Though . . . it's never really a thrill. Oh, this is more Michael's field. Don't you think, Lee? Michael's so good with metaphors."

"That's the vinegar talking," Lee said.

Martin said, "I'd be lost without my circus. And I also have a wife and son." He laughed. "I'm going home." He said good night.

"That wine will make you sick," Dad told me as he patted my shoulder. Then he excused himself for bed.

Lee said, "So only you got to enjoy the wine."

I thought of the day after my wedding, how Lee and I had almost argued at the marina. I thought of my work, how I faked interest in what now seemed like a frivolous business. I thought of Lee's work, how I played confidante to his ambition. I drank the wine from his glass. He had us defined. We were a young working couple with a young working marriage. He had us packed into a mold. He had everything so well fitted. His suits, his shirts, his waistband, our future. I thought I should shock him: I should buy him an oversized shirt.

Later, we made love. Soon after, he fell asleep, and I felt cut off from him. I stared at him for a while. I wanted to wake him, but instead I got up.

I called Cora in New York to tell her I was pregnant. She told me I shouldn't tell anyone until after my first trimester. Then she said, "Mom just cleaned out the insides of all the den clocks."

I said, "I'm coming home."

The next day was Friday. I drove to the Santa María store and passed new factories. Bulldozers were cutting away at a mountain to lay the foundation for a highway. The inside of the mountain was a brick color; it reminded me of a raw cut.

Part of the supermarket was also under construction. A delicatessen was being built. Color photographs hung from the ceiling in every aisle. I walked down the fruit juice aisle. I looked up at a photograph of apples, oranges and grapes. A clerk was on a ladder, lowering the photograph. The clerk glanced my way and smiled. The employees, both men and women, wore blue and white uniforms. Each employee took a supermarket etiquette course. If a cashier seemed dissatisfied with his or her job, my father would ask him or her if he could do anything to improve the job. He joked with them. Some admired him for it.

I started up another aisle. I thought of how often Lee sought refuge under the fluorescent lights and among the employees, strangers who were paid to show respect to him. Work for him, I realized, was not so much a challenge as it was a relief. He felt more confident at his job than he did at home.

A stock girl said hello to me. Two of the twelve cashiers were counting food stamps. A tape was playing a woman's melodic voice. She was announcing the day's specials, first in Spanish, then in English. *Viernes Social* was the busiest day for Dad's circle of friends. I recognized a friend of Dad's. I saw an old friend of Mom's. Mom's friend was putting several cans into her cart. I turned to go down another aisle. At the end of it, a Puerto Rican man held a young boy's hand. The man was signing a petition to keep the stores open Sunday.

That week, Lee was in the dairy section. He was rotating departments. If he stayed on the island, he'd become front end manager for six months. Then he'd work in the office as assistant district manager. If he returned to New York, he'd work on new business. He told me he'd make up his mind soon. I thought: without asking me.

I saw him. He was writing on a pad. He had one foot on a box near the dairy case. I asked him if he wanted to take a drive. I said, "There's a waterfall I used to go to, near the rain forest. I'll drive if you're too tired."

He drove. We were quiet. Without his sunglasses, he squinted. The sun was bothering his eyes. But he'd also become a little nearsighted.

I said, "Why don't you wear your glasses?"

"Because my eyes are fine." He glanced at the gas and the oil two or three times. We passed trucks, the backs filled with oranges and pineapples. Dogs walked along the side of the road.

"So many stray dogs," I said, staring at the mutts.

"Too many only to people like us," he said.

The traffic was bad. We were stuck in an intersection. And Lee said, "I went to a meeting of the New Progressive party today."

"But you don't even live here."

"Not important—the island can't stay like this. Independence is beneficial only in theory. To preserve the heritage, we need funds. We need statehood. It's not a perfect solution, but it's the best one around. And I can help; I'm an American who works here, someone with the power to help carry on old customs with improved methods."

"How will you help?"

"I'll raise money, maybe through Isla," he said. "Once I get your father going, the party will have more pull. We'll strengthen the economy and the culture."

I was enjoying his sudden enthusiasm for politics, in spite of its connection to his job. I said, "It sounds promising."

We went up a mountain on a road. The road was wide and paved. It used to be dirt and pebbles. The tops of palm trees joined in the air from both sides of the road. They formed a green tunnel. We passed a sign nailed to a tree: SE BEBE COCOS FRIOS / COLD COCOS. An arrow pointed to a path. Another sign, leaning on the porch of a house, said SE VENDEN CONEJOS.

Lee said, "No wonder we don't sell much rabbit at the stores. Look at our competition." He smiled as if to himself.

The houses were small, with corrugated tin roofs. Some had chickens near the front door. Some had plastic sheets instead of windows. We passed a cement house with a sign: IGLESIA PENTE-COSTAL. The church had no cross and the shutters were shut.

"Quiet up here," Lee said. He was squinting again. He reached into the glove compartment and took his sunglasses out.

We hit a fork in the road. I thought I knew by memory to turn right. But I didn't recognize anything. A *jibaro* was carrying bunches of plantains and bananas. He was short and wore a frayed straw hat. He stopped to watch the car pass. Lee parked the car off the road. He put the cassette deck and my purse into the trunk. Then he turned on the alarm.

"Why'd you want to come here?" he said.

"To walk with you. Where I used to walk."

Soon we were walking the same wooden steps I'd climbed years earlier. We reached the place where the waterfall had been. A stream was running through the trees and bushes. The boulders were dry. Beer cans were stuck between the rocks.

"Let's go to the national park," Lee said. "It's getting dark."

I said, "Let's go look at the view." We crossed the road. At the cliff, we saw houses and streets, lights turning on, shopping centers, ocean. "What was I thinking of when I dragged you here?"

"This?" He put his hands under my shirt. But then he stopped himself.

Later that night, I told Dad, "I may try to catch a plane tomorrow." We were at the pool. I was in the water.

"What's wrong?" He sat up in the lounge chair.

"Mom's not doing well. Cora's worried. I suppose I'm worried myself."

"Your mother sure knows how to make you run to her. Say, here comes Lee." He sounded relieved. "Your husband's a hard worker. Don't just fly away when he needs you."

Lee said, "Showers usually clear my head. But tonight I'm standing there calculating the loss we'd have annually if we shut down Sundays."

"Clarissa tells me she's thinking of going back to New York," Dad said, as if Lee had the right to change my mind. Dad took a cigar out of his shirt pocket. He held it out to Lee. "This usually helps clear my mind. And these aren't bad; they're Dominican."

I rolled off the raft, into the water. It was cold. I swallowed some water. Then I swam to the edge to get out. Dad was gone. Lee had put the cigar in his shirt pocket. He brought me a towel. "Why tell your father you're going home before telling me?" His look struck me; it was without a doubt sad.

"I was going to tell you."

He said, "You'll rest, we'll apologize, and we'll have a child. And then what?"

I dried my arms.

He said, "Clarissa, then what?"

"I don't know if we should have a child," I said. I walked to the house.

On my way to New York, I put on the headphones to listen to music. Haydn's "Surprise" Symphony was ending, and a selection of fugues from Bach's *Die Kunst der Fuge* began. The program was called "The Quieter Masterpieces." I thought of María and Julio and the record I'd given them. When my father had given *Die Kunst der Fuge* to me, he'd whistled the theme of the piece. He'd been off key. I thought of the score folded up in the album jacket.

Was I listening to the fourth canon now? I wasn't sure. I hadn't heard the fugues in over two years. They still pleased me. They were instructive. But they didn't sound that way. I admired how one theme had so many variations. I admired how each fugue stood on its own, yet at the same time all the fugues were related to one another. The last fugue kept coming into my head. I thought of its sudden drop into silence. Somehow that end resonated with me.

I was staring out the window, trying to remember my favorite arrangements of *Die Kunst der Fuge*. Instead, I remembered my second date with Lee. I'd said to him, "Do you like Bach?" He'd said, "My father likes Bach." At that time, Lee listened to rock 'n' roll. He liked Led Zeppelin. He recited to me the first few lines of their song "Stairway to Heaven": *There's a lady who's sure all that glitters is gold . . . and she's buying a stairway to heaven . . . when she gets there she knows if the stores are all closed . . . with a word she can get what she came for . . .* I wanted Lee to think I liked the song more than I did. So I said, "Doesn't that song begin with a pretty guitar solo?" And he said, "That's a deceiving solo. The song gets frantic." I remembered wondering whether or not he considered "frantic" to be a good thing. And was he one of those people who mistook frenzy for passion? I never asked him. But after we were married, I saw that for Lee frantic had nothing to do with passion. He knew one kind of passion and that was restrained and reserved for his work. As for the song, he'd only meant it was fast.

The selections from *Die Kunst der Fuge* were over. The final fugue hadn't been among them. I could see the tip of the airplane wing moving through a few thin clouds. But below the plane lay a bed of thick clouds. It looked lovely, as if there were two skies.

After Bach

By 7:00 A.M., I'd changed the mare's bedding. The stables were quiet and almost still, the way I loved them. As I began to curry the mare's velvety coat, I thought of what Michael had said to me the night before about Clarissa: "She'll be a cautious mother." But what if she was too cautious as our mother was? . . . The morning light came through the stall window and onto the mare's ass. My strokes were strong and circular. The mare was chestnut-colored, with a white spot on her forehead, and her name, predictably, was Star. I preferred the name Millicent. Ever since I'd started mucking out the stalls at the Riding Academy—a stable and ring in a garage on the West Side of Manhattan—I'd renamed each horse. Firefly became Henry; Rascal became Caesar; Princess became Maya; and Star, Millicent. I said "Millicent" twice to the mare as she started backing into a wall.

"Cora, call her Star; she'll know who you're talking to," the stable manager said. His name was Billy. He was thin and had dull red hair; he always wore a large silver cross. Several times he'd caught me talking to the horses; he seemed to enjoy sneaking up on me. I supposed that he liked me; he was always jittery when we spoke. I'd begun working for him as soon as I'd moved back in with Mother. The job was glorious, I thought, and I dreaded having to return to school in the fall.

"Star is a dull name," I said, combing the mare's mane.

"To a five-year-old child, it's perfect. . . . I have some good news: I'm promoting you to work in the office. You start Monday."

"Am I doing something wrong?" I sounded way too polite. "I like this job."

"Trouble is you like it too much. You're too slow. Anyway, I've already hired a guy to take your place. Star won't miss you, Millicent won't miss you." He petted the horse.

I was quiet; I combed the mane again.

"By the way," he said, "you'll make five bucks more an hour."

That brought me up to twelve dollars an hour. Maybe if I never bought anything and never ate out, by the end of the summer I'd have enough money to pay half of a first-month rent on my own place. I wanted Mother or Father to help me pay for an apartment. I'd pay them back; I'd get two jobs. But I was sure neither one of them would give me a start unless I finished college.

Billy came closer and said, "I didn't mean to upset you."

"I'm fine, really. Thank you for the opportunity." I hoped he'd leave me alone.

"I'll also give you a few free lessons," he said. "And by the way, call me whatever you want."

At home that night, Mother said to me, "You should be sent to London, to Switzerland, somewhere far away, to become a young lady. But no, you're shoveling manure."

"I've always wanted to go somewhere distant."

"Your sarcasm is very unbecoming. I'm going to call these

stables and tell the owner you can't work there anymore." Then she added, "Do take a shower before you sit in my house."

I didn't want to tell her about the promotion; she'd think I got it for her. I said, "Fine. Without a job, I'm free to go live with Dad."

She knocked over the umbrella stand and almost twisted her ankle. Oh, I knew how to rile her, yet she knew how to frighten me.

A few days earlier, I'd come home and found her in the den. She was busy at the desk, the cuckoo clock in front of her. She'd taken it apart. An open bottle of Lysol stood by the clock. With a sponge, she was cleaning the wheels and the weights. She said, without looking up, "Did you know cuckoos like to drop their eggs into another bird's nest? They like to use hawks. And the hawk raises their children."

"I didn't know that about cuckoos." I was frightened the wrong response would provoke her into hurling a clock across the room. I never wanted to think she was mad. I looked for a reason for her behavior: why not Father's rejections, dismissals and maybe even his confidences? As I thought of Father, I missed him and how, almost reverently, he'd set the clocks each month. I said, "Mother, you're ruining them."

"Nonsense; they've already been neglected."

Clarissa left Puerto Rico as soon as she could. She came straight to Mother's from the airport. She was tan and wore a long-sleeved loose white dress. Michael came over, too. He was living on West Ninth Street, in a small, untidy studio. I envied his privacy. He looked fit as ever, wearing khakis and one of Father's old work shirts, with a frayed shoulder seam. He was Chebutykin the doctor in *Three Sisters*, at the drama school of New York University. The last time I'd visited him, I noticed he'd checked out several anatomy books from the library. A stethoscope was draped over his chair; how diligent, I told him. He said, proudly, that he listened to his own heartbeat in the morning.

We were in the living room, waiting for Mother to call us for dinner. Clarissa sat at the piano, playing a Bach prelude—rather beautifully, I thought.

Michael said, "This assault on Dad's clocks—maybe it's because of their wedding anniversary. Which is—in case you've forgotten—just two days away."

"It's not that simple, and I'm scared," I said.

"She wants to scare you," he said. "It's her power."

Clarissa, still playing, whispered, "Amazing, how little I remember . . ."

She took her hands off the keys just as Mother shouted from the dining room hall, "Children! Come here and help me!"

I said, lightly hitting the piano leg, "Someone help *us.*"

We went into the hall.

Mother was taking out Father's wine bottles from the closet cellar. Her hair—she'd just washed and set it—was shorter, at her earlobe, and curlier. I'd snipped it that short. The style accented her high cheekbones; it made her look younger yet more severe. She said, "We're celebrating because we're together." She gave two bottles of wine to me, three to Michael, and two to Clarissa. "Carry as many as possible. I want to turn this cellar into a storage closet for all the things I'm tired of looking at."

Michael said, as if to himself, "Why'd he leave them all?"

"Maybe he cares less about them than everyone thinks he does," I said softly.

"I'll tell you why," Mother said and she was excited. "So we can look at all the gems he bought for no one but himself. . . . Put them all on the windowsill. Let's look at them in the light."

We lined as many bottles as we could on the long windowsill in the dining room. Soon I found myself arranging the bottles; I then insisted Michael do the same. All the Médocs were to stand to the right; next to them, the Saint-Émilions. I said to Clarissa, "It'd be best to combine the Graves and the Pomerols and set them over here."

She said, "Dad never mixed them."

I thought: This pretty arrangement should please Mother. It should also please Father: I've displayed every bottle so lovingly; I've relied on everything I've learned from him. Then I wondered if somehow I could please Penn with the display. I was acting ludicrous, I told myself, and then remembered the time Father had shown Penn how to hold a wineglass: "Take it by its stem, so the glasses clink together when we toast. Wine should appeal to all our senses, our sense of hearing, as well."

Michael pointed out that there were only two wines from Pomerol. Grinning, he put in a few Burgundies. The bottles gently knocked against one another. They were dusty and Michael wiped his hands on his pants. Father had only a few bottles of Chablis and Pouilly-Fuissé; so for variety, I interspersed the white wines with the red and placed the rest of the Burgundies on the floor.

Clarissa said, "Where does a Lafite go? That's over here—" She almost made a bottle fall.

"Wait," I said. "You're talking about a Classified Growth. That should go in the center. But where are the others? He had more."

Michael handed me some other bottles. He was no longer smiling. I heard Mother rattling something in the hall. The sun was setting, its rays streaming through all the colored glass. The white-wine bottles refracted some of the light, sending yellow beams in several directions across the wooden floor. The rest of the rays, shining through the red-wine bottles, cast one wide shaft of rose light under the dining room table.

We were drinking a delicious Château Margaux, 1959. Mother held up her glass. Cheerfully, she said, "It's so sad how quickly we all disperse. Overnight, it seems." She drank fast. "Michael, love, carve the roast beef. You're the expert."

What a pleasant mood she'd settled into.

Michael cut off a piece and ate it; he then sliced the beef in thick strips. "The end for Cora, the pink for Mother, and the pinkest for Clarissa."

Clarissa served the string beans and potatoes, putting each in a triangle on the plate, not one touching the other. She said to Michael, "How's the play going?"

"I don't feel one way or the other about it. Sidney Lumet's supposed to give a talk next week. Maybe he'll tell me how to feel."

"He did *Clockwork Orange,* right?" Clarissa said. "Ask him about the ending. I don't understand its neatness, something like: I was cured."

"Stanley Kubrick directed that. And it's not such a neat ending; it's an ill-suited one," Michael said.

Mother was neither eating nor listening. She was flushed from one glass of wine. I figured she was thinking of some past glory, maybe even her first anniversary. Then she blinked, refolded the napkin on her lap and said, "Why did you come home so soon, Clarissa?"

"I've already told you, it's a project at work." Her lie sounded convincing enough. "Lee's very busy anyway. He's getting involved with the Progressive Party. I think he plans on meeting the governor through Dad."

Mother said, "You may end up moving to that pitiful island. What an enormous debt they'll have one day, and such a small island, too. . . . But I'll stop at that. I've always said dinner is no place for politics."

Definitely, she was in an agreeable mood. I thought: This may be a wonderful time to suggest my getting my own place.

"Very tender roast beef," Michael said. He rubbed his forefinger along the rim of the wineglass until it screeched.

"Don't do that," Mother said. "As if you were two." She reached over to turn down the back of his shirt collar. "There. You are indeed a dashing young man."

This unasked-for gesture, this loving remark, reminded me of the days when she'd bought me silk nightgowns, warm socks and flannel robes. How many books had she given me? How many reruns had she watched with me? And she'd joked, always, about the doctors and their hospitals: how truly ridiculous they all were. As I watched her smooth her curls behind her ears, I longed to repay her. A gift . . . but what would she like? A recent photograph of everyone in the family, close together and smiling? I looked at the wine bottles on the sill; I thought of how the heat was damaging the wine. The sun had almost set, its dimming light like a mist around each bottle.

Mother was pushing the potatoes around on her plate. Then she dropped her fork on the table.

"Why aren't you eating?" I said.

"Funny, but I don't have much of an appetite. Such a waste, too." With her napkin, she wiped some fingerprints off the salt shaker. She tipped it over and didn't clean the salt up. "It's nice to hear you play again," she said to Clarissa. "What were you playing?"

"Bach, done poorly."

"Oh," Mother said, "that Bach."

I said, folding my hands on my lap, "Maybe I should get my own place. I'll get a full-time job—"

"You deserve a place of your own," Michael said.

Mother held her wrist as if to check the pulse of an arrhythmic heart. "What have I done now?"

"It's what I've done," I said, thinking of my job at the stables. "You disapprove."

Clarissa leaned forward and pleaded with her: "Don't you think you owe yourself more than playing with clocks—"

"Cora," Mother said, rubbing her wrists against the edge of the table, "are you telling lies about me?"

I drank my wine, thinking: I'm a fool. Two nights before her wedding anniversary is obviously not the time to talk about my wanting to move out. I'm a self-absorbed fool. My disease has made me too self-conscious. How despicable.

Mother said, "I'm always the one at fault in this family. As if I made Cora sick. I've given all my strength to caring for all of you, and not one of you ever acknowledges it."

I was certain of what she'd say next: why wasn't I grateful for her nursing me back to health?

She walked to the window. I worried she was going to sweep the bottles off the sill. Instead, she picked one up and said, "Your father was always trying to impress; and it's so unfair. There was that time . . ." She put the bottle down. Slowly, she took her cigarettes from the table and tried to light one, but she couldn't get the match lit. After several strikes, she lit the cigarette and then tossed the burned match and the matchbook onto the string beans on her plate. "He asked me to marry him. Yes, but let's be fair: there's more. . . . He also told me he had a daughter. And, Clarissa, that was you." She smoked her cigarette and stared out the window. The smoke drifted over the bottles.

I smiled nervously at Michael; Clarissa looked at me. We all had to be thinking the same thing: Mother did sound mad. Michael threw his napkin on the table. I stared at the match lying on the plate.

"Let's not talk about this right now," Clarissa said.

And Mother, stroking her white neck again and again, said, "I'm only telling you what happened. Please remember: I'm the one who told you."

After Mother shut herself in her bedroom (I checked on her; she seemed asleep), Michael left, forgetting his keys on the dinner table. Clarissa walked silently through the house: from the dining room she went into the kitchen, from the kitchen into the hall, from the hall into the den, where I sat, drinking the rest of the wine. She said, "I'm leaving. I can't be in her home anymore."

I surely wasn't going to stay there by myself. I took a cab to the stables. I didn't want to see anyone; I didn't want to speak to anyone. But Billy was in the office, drinking a beer and going through some old files. He'd made a mess on the desk. He said, "You haven't come back to groom the horses again."

"Maybe I have."

He laughed and walked me to Millicent's stall. I stroked her neck; soon my hand was lined with chestnut hair. Why the hell was Billy here so late?

"Cora, what's wrong?"

"My mother hates that I work here."

"Is that so?" He finished his beer and immediately crushed the can. "I was never able to do that before." He looked at the can and then tossed it into the trash.

I locked my hands around Millicent's neck in a final stage of an exercise called Emergency Dismount. I swung on her neck for a second until she shook me off. Then the mare gracefully lowered her head for me to pet. "I wish I could ride her now."

"Saddle her up," Billy said. "I'll give you lesson number three, which is much more fun than the first two."

We took the mare into the ring; I got up on her. Billy told me to ask her for a trot. I posted. He was sweet: he commended me on my ease. He said, "Excellent. Now canter around. Feel her rhythm; it's a little jerky. Then, when you're used to her, I'll show you something nice." He sat on a stool in the corner of the ring.

After I'd cantered around the ring four times, I slowed down to a walk. Feeling shy, I said to him as I passed, "Thanks for this."

He rolled up his sleeves. He said, "Okay, let go of the reins. Feet out of the stirrups. Get her into a very steady walk." He was following me. "Now hands out to the sides, balance yourself, good. . . . Close your eyes."

I obeyed. What a sensation: this animal gently guiding me through the darkness. My breathing was steady and loud. I heard, "Keep going, lean back a little, relax the shoulders a bit."

Relax? Not an easy thing, for I was picturing Mother in front of the window, a wine bottle touching her hip. What had she been thinking? Nonsense, apparently, because Clarissa was so much like her. Wasn't she? She had Mother's expressions . . . but I looked more like Mother. Clarissa looked like Father. I was trembling. I opened my eyes.

"Hey, no looking. Keep going. Get her into a trot and hold on with your thighs."

This was getting difficult. My legs hurt. I thought of Penn and of boys I'd known after Penn, who all seemed to have as much impact on me as I'd allowed Billy to have. Then I resented—as Mother had come to fiercely—the uncompromising impulse of loving one person.

"Okay, Star's had enough," Billy said. He applauded me. "Haven't you?"

*   *   *

. . . maybe I'm not her son either. Why couldn't she just say:
You have no mother, my dear Clarissa . . . ?

Always acted as if she wanted baby after baby, as if . . . as if
she's been making up for someone once having not wanted her.
Her mother? Father? Oh, Michael, I was a war child, remember,
running from roof to roof, and my father sang to me every night,
and my mum, before the war, gave me pudding.

Fifty-eighth, fifty-ninth, bridge, sixtieth, rhythm of tires,
rhythm of cracks.

Did she ever want to be anything else? Never asked. Did I?
Oh, yes, Michael a ballerina . . . But imagine me, your mother,
caught half naked on that stage! Be caught?

Right above me, behind lit windows, child born every few
seconds. Need a home. Warm home, but not with a liar. Two
liars. Two of a kind, two peapods, how's it . . . ? Left my keys.
Where to go? I'll call you. But what's the time? In San Juan?
Hour later. One time proves another false.

I took Lee's car. I drove toward Montauk. I wanted to go to the
lighthouse there. I thought of Mom's story. It wasn't true. She
was furious with Dad, with Cora, with me. But I knew she'd love
to raise an unwanted child. So maybe it was true. Then who was
my mother? And so what if it was true? I passed West and then
East Hampton. I felt my belly. I got to Montauk Point and
parked on a road near the ocean.

I couldn't find the lighthouse. I found the beach. I stepped
through weeds. There was a half-moon. I took off my shoes and
my socks. I wanted Lee beside me. I almost felt his hand under
my own. Lee's palm was smooth. I used to rub palms with him as
if both hands belonged to the same body. The sand felt hard.
The water was cold, too cold, and it numbed my feet. I was
shivering. I started walking back to the car.

A car was parking near mine. A teenager, who looked about
seventeen, came out of the car. He said to me, "Hey, careful. It's
a strange night." He wore a polo shirt, a cardigan and khaki
shorts. "Tide's high. Moon's low," he said. He was drunk. A girl

giggled behind him. She put her arms around his chest. Behind her, another boy was taking off his shoes. They all seemed to be home from prep school. They all reeked of marijuana.

"You from here?" the girl said to me.

"Not at all."

"How's the water?" That was another's voice.

I spotted the lights of houses up the road. "The water's good," I said. I walked away.

I got into the car, and the seat felt hot. My thighs stuck to the leather. A few minutes later, I ran out of gas. I turned on the hazard lights, left the car and said aloud, "Lee would've checked the fuel, the oil, all the vital signs."

I didn't want to call him. Mom's story, whether true or false, had nothing to do with Lee. I wanted to keep the information as my own. If only for a while.

I headed toward a lit house. I knocked on the door and a heavy man in a checked bathrobe answered. "I'm sorry to wake you," I said, "but I ran out of gas. May I call a tow truck?"

"Have you been swimming? That's plain crazy in this cold at this hour," he said, his voice rough. He cleared his throat. "Come in," he said, "but be quiet. The son's sleeping. Any other day, I'd have given you the extra gas in the garage, but you're out of luck. I used it myself today. How'd in hell's name you run out of gas? Busted gauge?"

"Maybe not," I said and looked around his home. He used clam shells as ashtrays. He had two rocking chairs with broken wicker seats. A swordfish was mounted on the wall. As he took me to the phone, I asked the man where I was. "No close station, is there?" I said after I'd made my call.

"Not at this hour," he said. He was now eating potato chips. "Wait here if you want. You look cold, miss." He offered me a chip. He said he loved snacks.

"I'll just get back to the car." I took a few chips and said, "I had a light dinner."

"Sorry I was so gruff before." He handed me the bag of chips. He told me to finish them and then said, "I'm a bear when I wake up. I am sorry. But I'm warning you: the truck'll be late. The

truck's always late." He turned to the fish on the wall and said,
"Hey, did you ever see one of these?" He clapped his hands. The
fish began to wriggle as if suddenly doused with water.

"Clever," I said. I ate chip after chip.

"Very clever, eh? Looks dead and then at a clap of the
hands . . ."

I left him and walked to my car. I crumpled the empty chip
bag and turned on my headlights. Up the road I saw a car swerve
around my own and halt. Someone got out. I heard a boy yell,
"No way. I'm not driving with this guy anymore." As he passed
me, he said, "You were right. The water was real cold, but it felt
good." His friends drove away.

"I ran out of gas," I said and stepped out of the car and closer
to the teenager. He was the one who'd been taking off his shoes.
The boy's hair was black, wet and long. A piece of hair stuck to
his cheek. In the glow of the headlights I saw he had blue eyes
and black eyebrows. He had white skin. He wore jeans and an
old Dartmouth sweatshirt, stained with ink.

"Did you call a tow truck?" he said. He walked me to the car.
"I can't ride with my friend when he's drunk. The guy's been in
two accidents. Do you care if I wait with you?"

I said, "I guess you're from around here." I opened the car door
so I could look at him in more light. He was a little unshaven.
He looked angelic when he smiled. One front tooth overlapped
the other.

"Yeah, my family has a beach house nearby. But I'm off to
Bowdoin College—heard of it? You finish one level of school and
they send you off to the next. But I have nothing against education. It's a fine way to get scared of the world."

It was becoming colder. I got in the car. I threw the potato
chip bag on the floor. The boy got in without my asking him. He
said, "Why are you here all alone?"

Why wasn't I scared? Because I knew this "type" of boy? I said,
"I'm visiting my mother."

He said, "I had to shoot my dog this morning. He was hit by
a truck and convulsing bad, real bad. I'd never used a gun before.
It was my father's rifle. And I didn't miss."

"I'm sorry."

"I didn't miss. I'm sorry there was a bullet in the gun. See, I didn't know that my father used it. Looks like he uses it, and I don't even know what for." He nodded yes as if to emphasize his point.

"You sound kind of Southern," I said. "Some words, they sound—"

"That's fake. Do you like it?"

"I suppose, I suppose, I suppose I like it," I said.

"You have one dimple. I've never seen a one-dimpled smile before."

"What a sheltered life."

"So we're alone," he said. "And so maybe I should go. 'Cause I think I want to sit here and kiss. And who am I to do that with you? A soaked eighteen-year-old. I'll just go." He opened the door. "The truck'll be here soon."

"Wait with me," I said.

He ran a finger along the dashboard. He reached across my lap and pressed open my door. "Let's get out," he said.

I did. I shut the door behind me. I leaned against the car. He leaned against me; I felt how hard he was. He kissed me and I didn't move. His touch was light. He felt my wedding band. He paused and then slipped off his pants. He wasn't wearing shorts. I was ashamed and almost sick. He raised my arm a little to prod against my hip. He said, "Let's keep your clothes on." He kept pressing against my hip. He didn't try to get inside me. I didn't want to make a sound, but I did. Then the boy came on Lee's car. He said, his head against my shoulder, "Did you like it?" Then he leaned against me, completely, without hugging, until he stopped trembling. I straightened up and looked at the boy. I saw Lee in my mind. The boy ruffled his hair. He put his clothes on and squatted. He bounced on his heels once and lit a cigarette. He closed one eye every time he exhaled.

I glanced at the tires, the fender, the window and the steering wheel.

He walked up to me. "Can I kiss . . . ?"

"It'd be better if you left."

*　　*　　*

It was two days after Montauk, almost the end of my week's vacation. I'd phoned Dad to tell him what had happened with Mom. He told me he was coming to New York for business. He said he'd come in earlier, to see me. We were in his suite at the Plaza. The room overlooked Central Park. He was looking at himself in the mirror. He wore a jacket, no tie, and sneakers. He said, "Well, well, you're pregnant. It's your turn as a parent; you'll be fine."

He'd ordered lunch. Chicken salad, shrimp salad, fruit salad, nut breads, white wine. He helped himself to some fruit salad.

I said, "Is this the room you always get?"

"They gave me the honeymoon suite; they said they were booked. . . . These kiwis look good, Clarissa."

I paced the room, which, for the moment, felt smaller. Someone fumbled with keys outside our door. I said, "I wish we could be home."

He poured himself a glass of wine. He said, "What are we missing? We have the park outside our window, we have treats." He took out two books on advertising from his suitcase. "I thought you'd like these."

I thanked him and leafed through one book. He was making a plate of food for me. I walked into the bathroom. There was a phone there. Now I wanted to call Lee. I still hadn't talked to him since I'd left Puerto Rico three days earlier. I wanted him to leave work and come to me. Then I thought of the boy at the beach and didn't like how much his image distracted me. I went back to my father. He was helping himself to more fruit salad.

I was angry at having to begin. "So talk to me," I said. "Mom told us some story. Maybe it's a true story. . . . She's giving away all your wine; she's ruining all your clocks."

He stared at his fork. He said, "I cannot make her better."

I wanted him to tell me a flawless tale, to justify Mom's behavior. Or I wanted him to lead me to my real mother. His calmness kicked at me.

He said, "Don't you want anything to eat?"

I said I wasn't hungry.

"I haven't talked about your mother in a very long time. You look like her. And you use your looks to advantage as she did."

"Who is she?"

He wiped his mouth several times. He looked different to me. But I couldn't tell what had changed. He said, "How about some mineral water?" He got up to call room service. Once off the phone, he told me the hotel had ten kinds of mineral water.

Angry, I said, "Will you just sit with me?"

"I'm sorry." He sat. "Your mother's name was Amelia Eliot." He laughed a little to himself. Just then it seemed to me he was always laughing a little to himself. "I must like the briskness of British women," he said. "She was from a fine British family. They'd moved to Boston for business. She died there, too." He sounded hurt. For her? for me? for him? If for him, that seemed new.

He took off his jacket. He seemed more than hurt. I was certain he was hearing my mother's voice. But he was telling me only what he wanted to. He said, "She was engaged, you see; otherwise, I would have married her. And that was it, really: I met her on Bat Island, and I went there a lot to be with her."

"Why didn't she want to marry you?"

"The Eliots were very Catholic . . . very selective about which rules they could disregard." He shifted his weight in the chair. He'd been too quick with that reply. Then he said, "She was the one who left me. To this day, I can picture her, vividly. She was small; and she played the piano . . . not like you, not as well." He took a sip of wine.

"May I have some water?" I said.

"Where's that mineral water?" He opened the ice bucket. He used his fingers instead of the tongs and dried each fingertip on a paper napkin.

I sorted out his story. One, my mother had been forbidden by her parents to marry a Jew. Or two, she'd used her religion as an excuse. Or three, she'd loved her fiancé. Or four, she was deceiving my father. But what did this mother mean to me? I could see what she meant to my father. He'd preserved his memory of her, his love, too, by lying to me. He looked anguished. That was what I'd never seen in him before. I'd probably never feel such anguish for Lee, I thought. Knowing Lee would never put me in the position to feel it calmed me.

My father gave me a glass of water. "I met Julia very soon after your mother stopped seeing me."

"And you believe I'm yours?" I poured some water on the table.

"I believed Amelia." He was speaking evenly. "You're my blood; there's no doubt of that. . . . The night she called me from Boston, she was already eight months pregnant. As soon as her fiancé had found out about you, he left her; and her father wanted nothing to do with her. . . . She was sick those last few months. She told me that she'd been advised not to have children. Something to do with her heart. But she wanted you, she said, for me. Then she died while giving birth to you. And what was I to do?"

I was tearing the label off the wine bottle. I asked him what else he wanted me to ask.

At a Crossing

It was early evening, and you and I were walking on the beach. You'd asked Clarissa, Cora and me to come to Bat Island—the invitation, your grand apology. But behind your remorse I thought you seemed pleased and I said, "You tried to keep things neat." As we walked, I picked up tiny shells and crushed them with my thumb and forefinger. Bat Island was dry from weeks without rain, the breeze was hot, and the roses along the town road had shrunken into fists. You looked sad, as if trapped in that somnolent place where memories are too sharp.

"Do you think she's crazy?" I said.

"Your mother is not at all crazy, even in her worst moments." Picking up a clump of seaweed, you tossed away some strands and kept some black pods, which you'd once told me were shark eggs. "She's a very free woman."

"And you're her one constraint."

"Not really," you said and pointed to a bat. "I once saw a film on bats. It showed a pallid bat in slow motion, catching a meal-worm. The bat somersaulted and then its wings folded over the worm like a cape. I wish we could see that grace."

The bat flew out of sight. Walking again, your hands deep in your pockets, you said, "You learn to live with some mistakes. You'll learn, too."

"Do you think that's good?"

"It'll be rotten," you said, "if your sister never forgives your mother and me."

The next day, Cora suggested we climb a cliff that looked gently sloped. She tied her T-shirt at the bottom, so her stomach showed. Clarissa put some sneakers on; earlier, in her bare feet, she'd stepped on a sea urchin. She said she'd rather just watch Cora and me. I started climbing, and right away I slipped. Cora, her blond hair almost whipping me in the ear, passed me, reaching the first level of flat rock, and she said, "Look at that."

I turned to see a familiar red dinghy in the water, carrying Mitchell Willet and a woman who looked like Mother.

Clarissa, from the ground, said, "Well, well, what a surprise."

Mitchell Willet and Mother, wearing a black straw hat, both walked onto the beach.

"Look at our luck, Mitch," Mother cried. "All three of my beauties."

Willet said, "A very good sign; the start of a wonderful holiday."

"What's he got going?" I whispered to Cora. And I thought: Mother had to face you, Father; she had to see if you'd detest her.

Clarissa helped Mother onto the shore and gave her a towel. While Mother was drying off her white calves, Clarissa sat on a rock and began drawing concentric circles in the sand.

"The spheres of music," I said to her.

"A circle of fifths," she replied, "my kind. They don't descend or ascend; they only echo."

Willet motioned Cora to come to the dinghy. "I have a friend here on the island," he said, "and she's asking about parachute skiing. Have you ever tried that?"

Cora looked at me. "Maybe Michael has; he's braver than I. . . . Have you guys seen my father, by chance?"

Mother, holding one sandal, wiped sand off her foot and said, "Let's not speak of your father. Let's talk about us. After that night . . . I know you're all so cross with me for doing what I did. We must talk. You'll come visit me at Mitch's house and we'll talk."

"Lee and I are leaving for Puerto Rico tomorrow night," Clarissa said.

I said, "You're very hospitable, Mitch."

At home that evening, Clarissa told you, "Mother's here with Mitchell Willet. On what she calls her 'holiday.' "

You were on the couch, reading *The Decline and Fall of the Roman Empire*. "With Willet?"

"Yes," Cora said, cracking pecans and offering them around the room. "Mom's so fond of games."

"I feel as if I haven't seen Julia in a long time," Lee said. He'd become more reticent around the family since Clarissa had found out about her mother.

"Julia won't bother us," you said, going back to your book, but you stayed on the same page for several minutes. "Did she say when she was leaving?"

In the morning, I wanted to go fishing, and crossing the bridge, I saw a woman with long black hair. As she passed me, she said, "Don't I know you?"

"I was thinking the same about you," I said, though it wasn't true. Her legs were white and strong, but her arms were thin. She had green eyes and wore a striped green sundress that was cut low, and I saw how white her breasts were. She looked about forty or a little older.

"I'm Anna-Marie Benton," she said, "and you're . . . ? Dav-

id's son! Yes, we met years ago, when you were much smaller."
Her grip was weak as she shook my hand. She wore a diamond
almost the size of a penny, and it had rubies around it. "What a
coincidence! I was going to phone your father tonight and see if
we could have dinner. I'm here with a friend. Do you know Eve
Shore? Eve and I have rented Rhia Wiston's house on the other
side of the island. So how's everyone?"

"Very good."

"Your mother was in town earlier with Mitchell Willet, of all
people. She certainly can bring a little light to Mitchell's life."
She laughed, a soft laugh.

We began walking together.

I said, "You've known my parents for years."

"Yes, I have a great deal of respect for your father." She
seemed pleased about that. "What does a teenager do here?
When I was sixteen, my friends and I used to take buses and
trains all over the place: Chicago, Detroit . . ." She was quiet
until I told her I wasn't a "doer," and then she said, "If I came
here a lot, I'd get a parachute. Mitchell says he's going to have
a ski boat with a parachute come over tomorrow. Eve doesn't
think I have the guts to go."

We walked south of the bridge toward the Fingers, where
Anna-Marie decided she wanted to fish. She'd never fished before; and so, hooking worms for her, I pretended to wait for
something to bite, but I knew there were no big fish around the
Fingers. We talked about a plane crash over Jost Van Dyke that
had killed all ten on board, about the randomness of such disasters, and then talked about the inbreeding of dogs, for she used
to have a Rottweiler with minor hip problems. We'd been talking for almost an hour, and now, staring at the water, she said,
"Are you sure there are fish around here? All I've ever seen are
snails."

"Minnows," I said. "May we meet again tomorrow? Early
evening, if you survive your jump?"

She stood, brushed her sandy palms against her shorts and
said, "I see your father has taught you to be a true gentleman."

"Oh, no, I learned all my social graces at school: graces of
dress, drugs, drinking and money."

"The graces of money? They're always amusing."

"You think so? I remember there was a girl who used to wear a pair of lizard gloves that cost over a thousand dollars. They reached her elbow and everyone thought she was hiding track marks."

Anna-Marie laughed and said, "Well, only a malcontent would flaunt what he or she buys; however, if you're used to certain luxuries, there's nothing wrong with letting people know. Otherwise, you're just playing the hypocrite, and that's a too-common thing."

I said, "Meet me tomorrow. Here at three. It'll give us both something to do."

The next morning, while you were reading the paper, I thought of how you never saved any of the articles written about the Isla charity balls for hospitals, orphanages and victims of earthquakes. You were reading about the first political kidnapping in Puerto Rico; someone had abducted the Chilean consul. Folding the paper, you said, "The other day I was having breakfast with the vice-president of Yes films and I started telling him about our shrink problem in the Virgin Islands. He says to me, 'I'm sorry to hear you have to send your employees to psychiatrists.' So I tell him that shrink is a loss from expected profits and that the stealing in the Virgin Islands is really hurting us. And it is, you know."

I said, "I suppose he had something to say about your quarterly analysis, too."

"Well, it was funny at the time."

Clarissa and Lee came into the kitchen, dressed alike in khaki shorts. Clarissa said, "Here's unexpected news: we're moving to Puerto Rico, after all. Lee says he'd like to be able to go to the stores whenever he pleases. He wants his employees to know he's always there for them. Yet another little surprise . . ."

"Why put it like that?" Lee said. "The truth is, if we're going to have a family, I don't want to have to leave you for several days just to go to work."

"The rents in Puerto Rico are so reasonable," you said and

began to prepare breakfast, using butter and whole milk for the scrambled eggs.

Cora came in, looking like a little girl, dressed in a long nightshirt, her eyes puffy from sleep. "What are you smiling about?" she said to you.

"Your father's happy," Lee told her and held out plates onto which you could dish out the eggs. "That's quite a thing: to make someone in this family happy."

"Happy?" Cora said. She went to get some sugar and then left the spoon in the cup and almost poked her eye each time she sipped.

"We're moving to Puerto Rico," Clarissa said. "I think I'll change jobs, too. Maybe I'll just be a mother."

"Let's all try to be mothers," Cora said. "Mother David, Mother Michael, Mother . . ." She walked out of the kitchen.

"If I were a mother, I'd cook my eggs with olive oil," Lee said, soaking up the yolk with his bread.

You went back to the paper, saying to Lee, "I was telling Michael, the other day I'm talking to the president of Yes films . . ."

When I came back from taking Clarissa and Lee to the seaplane, you and Cora were still in the kitchen, cleaning up. "I guess the plane took off on time," you said.

I said, "Did you hear someone come in?"

The kitchen door opened and there was Mother. She looked pretty in a knee-length red dress. It'd been two years since she'd seen you, and she blushed and said, "I'm sorry if I'm interrupting anything, but I . . . I can't stay with that man anymore. He's polite and he's kind, but he has a bird that's the size of a dog in his house and . . . and the truth of the matter is, Mitch is falling in love with me. Well, I can't have that—" She hurried to the counter and wiped off invisible crumbs, anything, it seemed, so as still not to look at you. "I know I've barged into my own home. But if I can't stay here, I've got to stay at that bloody hotel until I get a plane in the morning." She paused, then studied you. "You look well."

We were all quiet, steeped in that awkwardness that comes after a confidence is betrayed.

"Your mother and I have to talk," you said.

"We've nothing to hide from them," Mother said, now sitting at the table, her joined hands forming a triangle at her lips.

I left the kitchen anyway and sat in the living room, where every chair and pillow was in place.

The doorbell rang. I went to get it, hoping it'd be Anna-Marie, but it was Mitchell Willet, holding Mother's straw hat and looking disheveled in a creased linen suit. He said, "Is your mother here? She forgot this."

"I'll make sure she gets it."

"If you'd just tell her I'm here. It's important I talk to her."

I felt sorry for him—for his becoming involved with my family—so I went to get Mother.

"Why, Mitch," she said, "what is it?"

"You left some of your things at my house," he told her, handing her the hat. "I've arranged for a boat to take you back to San Juan, if you'd like."

"I won't take another boat, thank you," she said.

You walked out of the kitchen, dish towel and bowl in hand.

Willet looked surprised that you were home. "I see I was mistaken about our plans, Julia," he said. "I won't be needed, then." And he left, walking briskly down the path.

Drying the bowl, you went into the den and shut the door.

"That's straightened out," Mother said to Cora and me. She moved the pillows around on the couch, brushed off the coffee table and then sat on it, staring at the den door and playing with her hat.

Anna-Marie was on a motorbike by the bridge, her upper body stretched over the handlebars, her black hair not loose but braided. I told her Willet had dropped in unexpectedly, and she said she'd seen Willet and Mother that morning at the beach. "We didn't go parachuting, after all. I told Mitchell I didn't have the guts, and he said he'd order a boat tomorrow, just in case I found the courage. And then your mother slapped his hand."

"She hates impudence."

She dismounted the bike and began crossing the bridge, saying, "Are you like your mother?"

We headed for the forest, and I said, "You should see the bats at night. They're very graceful."

She sat under a tree and her shorts inched up her thighs. She looked as if she had somewhere to go. To get her to stay, I thought of telling her Clarissa's story or asking her whether she knew Amelia Eliot, but I said, "What does your husband do?"

"He's a photographer. He's in Guatemala, living in a hut. He's taking pictures of refugee children for his show this winter. I don't like huts. Paul, my husband—"

"Paul."

"Yes, he used to be a commercial photographer. That's how I met your father, as a matter of fact. Paul once did publicity work for Isla."

I flicked a beetle off Anna-Marie's hand.

She said, standing, "I should go. . . . How old are you? Eighteen, nineteen? You're a gloomy teenager. I'll give you a thrill: a ride back to the house."

Sitting behind her on the scooter, I said, "Let's have coffee in the city. Napoleons . . . do you like napoleons?" She laughed and I smelled the scent of soap and soil on her neck. "Here's good," I said to a spot that was far from the house. I walked away and then turned and yelled, "You're making a mistake! Keep riding and it'll become an irreversible mistake. . . ."

She rode back to me and said, "You're getting too wild."

But I felt that she liked my temper. The motorbike tilted under her, she said, "Listen, I'm not unhappily married. But I do know how to enjoy myself. Which makes me think I'm not your type at all. But you flatter me. Now, if I do call you, promise me: no fuck-ups. That's a promise you'll have to keep."

When I returned to the house, all the lights were out except for a lamp under which Cora lay sprawled on the couch, cracking more nuts and reading the paper. She said to me, "Mom's been in the tub an hour. This island . . ." She threw me a nut. "A certain kind of person fits in perfectly here. Mother, Mitchell Willet, even me . . . Solitude becomes the three of us. I, for one, feel more comfortable with fewer and fewer people. Dad says Mitchell Willet has very little faith in people and that's what made him such a vicious businessman." She threw the bag of nuts on the table.

Mother called for her, asking for some iced tea. Cora got her the tea, came back to the living room and said, "She keeps draining out a little bit of water and then refills the tub with hot water. Her skin's pink."

"I don't know why you wait on her." But I didn't want to fight—I was in a fine mood—so I said, "I think you need a swim."

We left to go diving off the lowest cliffs.

When we got back, you were near the door, picking up a leaf someone had carried into the house. You said, "Your mother fell asleep in the water."

"What are you going to do now?" Cora said.

"Don't look so scared." You bent down to push your toe through a hole in your slipper. "These slippers are finished."

"I must ask you something, David," Mother said, quietly drifting into the room, wearing your sweatshirt, and I admired her for having manipulated your anger into pity. "That Amelia Eliot— you knew her from here? Why didn't I ever see that this small island was of some monumental importance to you? So this is where you met that Amelia—"

"Mitchell Willet told you that?" you said. "What a blessing he is. . . ."

"Leave that be. He's not here anymore." She sat on the couch. "Dear god, the horrors we live with: imagine a woman dying while giving birth. How can such a wondrous moment, one that should be celebrated and applauded, become such an unforgettable tragedy? I haven't thought of this in years, but what a sight—all those children, in that courtyard, all those children."

"What are you talking about?" you said.

"There were all these children in a courtyard, destroyed by the

war, hungry, without mothers, running around half naked. . . .
I didn't know what they were looking for. . . . I was behind the
gate on my way home, watching, and Mum said never to stare,
but the children were so much younger than me. I knew I'd be
late, and I ran home, to find out my mum had died just that
morning, and my father was tearing apart her closet, from her
one pair of silk gloves to her sturdy boots for planting, tearing it
all apart. He'd never forgive her for going so suddenly, I saw
that." She stopped to look at the ceiling fan. "I wasn't there for
him. I thought he didn't want me; he'd take me to the yard and
leave me with all those children."

You said, "Stop acting like this! You're not mad."

Cora began to cry, and Mother held her, saying, "No more
crying, no more."

I walked to the window and touched the bat screen you'd put
up when we first moved in. "You try to keep the bats out," I said,
"but the truth is nothing wants to come in here. It stinks in here.
Something is rotting in this house. Don't you think, Father?
Maybe it's your good faith."

You looked at me for some time and then said, "There's nothing wrong with you. Michael, there's nothing wrong with any of
us."

I wasn't tired, but I was lying on my bed, in my jeans, thinking
of you, then thinking of Anna-Marie and her telling me, Promise me: no fuck-ups. She could have put it more politely, but
no. . . .

I heard a loud horn; I heard it again. It sounded like the siren
of a boat, and I got up and went to the terrace. The wind was
bending the trees, and I saw that the Fingers were on fire. The
smoke was rising and spreading across the east side of the island.

I went into the den. You were already in there, dressed. You
said, "They're going to need help." A car was coming to the
house. "And here they are," you said, putting on your shoes;
everyone else was still asleep, Mother in the guest room.

Looking out the window, I saw Martha Megran drive up in

Terrence's car. I met her at the door and you were behind me.

"There's a horrible fire," she said. "Mitchell's trying to calm everyone, but—"

"I'm on my way," you said and got into the Jeep.

As you were driving away, Mother came out, holding her robe together with her hands, the belt dragging on the floor, and she said to Martha, "Dear, we must stick together. I'll get Cora, we'll throw on some clothes, and you'll drive us to the fire."

"I can feel the heat already," Cora said. The sky looked yellow, and a light ash fell on us as we got closer to the fire. We were still a few miles away but saw how quickly the woods and the brush around the caves were burning and how the flames sent flashes of light over the water. The bats shrieked, flying in all directions until they formed a stream in the sky, moving south.

We parked near the bridge, which the firemen were destroying so the flames wouldn't spread to the other side of the island. Behind the caves I saw a fireboat, spraying water onto the caves, but one boat wasn't enough, and there was little time for any more help to come from the neighboring islands. Willet was standing near the bridge, and his gleaming head reflected the brightness of the fire.

"Mister Willet, I warned you about those kids hanging around by the caves," the pharmacist Tack was saying. "The other boat got away. The boy we caught didn't know the waters, otherwise he'd also be long gone." With his hands, Tack shielded his eyes from the flames.

Terrence, hitting his cane against a palm tree, said to me, "We'll have the boy hung."

"The fireboat isn't doing much good," Mother said. "Why is it that all the things that are supposed to do good don't?"

And Martha, holding a goatskin flask, told her, "Those boys should stay home. Set their own huts on fire."

Anna-Marie and her friend Eve Shore rode toward us on their motorbikes. They parked and hurried over to Mitchell Willet. Anna-Marie then went up to you, holding her black hair in a bun while she spoke. I imagined you were feeling steady again, saying how tragic it was: one human blunder and the bats flee, not to return for months, years.

Then you said to Willet, "What a mess."

"But we know how to smother our fires," he said and walked away.

Cora and I were watching Tack, who was now leading a boy to Willet's Jeep. The boy was about sixteen and had his head down.

I was watching Anna-Marie, coming closer, making my heart quicken, and she said to me, "Are you okay? Eve and I were drinking champagne on the terrace, and we could smell the smoke all the way over there. It smells like singed fur."

Now she's glancing at you with what kind of eyes—knowing? collusive? Lady, oh, lady, kindly wash your hands of all but me. There she goes: move the hair, as if it feels so good. Reminding herself just how good by touching.

She whispered to me, "Look how gorgeous the sky is: all lit up."

Mother was able to get on a seaplane back to Puerto Rico that afternoon. After she said goodbye to Cora, she said to you, "Call me in Santa María; I'll stay there for a few days."

And to keep her calm, I thought, you said you would.

I drove her to the marina. She sat in the front seat, going through her purse. Her hair was blown back, showing me how little her face had aged, and she leaned closer to me so I could hear her in the wind: "I'm all set. I have my wallet, my keys, my photographs, everything I need. . . . But you can be sure I'll forget one thing—all this hurt; we protect ourselves by forgetting. You'll be there to see me forget, won't you, my baby?"

And like you, I said yes.

Part Three

---❦---

A Second Forest

By the winter of 1980, I'd been living on Bat Island for several months. I'd just turned twenty-one. Clarissa and Michael both told me how much they envied my life; they said it was idyllic. Maybe it was. Mitchell Willet had taught me how to garden and landscape. His strength and dexterity surprised me. So did his kindness. Soon I was eager to help him replant the east side of the island. We'd walk along the shore there. We'd stumble on deposits of ash and kick up bits of charcoal. Though grasses and herbs were rapidly sprouting, there were many patches of burned grass, which the sun beat into a dull gold. "Plant seed wherever you want," Mitchell said to me one afternoon. "The wilder it is the more difficult it'll be for people to walk through the forest and get to the caves. There's no use trying to prevent another fire; actually, the fire has enriched the soil. Most natural disasters are slow renewals. That's the genius of nature." He walked to the

edge of the Fingers; he stared for some time at the barren ground.
He said, "And you can be sure the bats will return."

He ordered saplings. They arrived with many sacks of soil by
boat. We took everything in a truck (the bridge having been
rebuilt in iron) from the marina to the caves. The mature trees
arrived by air—banana, palm, bamboo. For over two weeks,
helicopters and small planes hovered noisily over the east side of
the island.

On weekends, Mitchell and I met for afternoon tea and scones
on his porch. One night, he told me, "Your family has a quiet
fighting spirit. I like that, but it's too quiet to resolve the larger
problems."

Pluto, his white cockatoo, pecked at a dish of seeds from a
perch.

"That's exactly why they keep it so quiet," I said, throwing a
piece of scone on the floor near the bird.

Father called me frequently; Mother wrote me as many as four
letters a week. She said talking to me and Clarissa over the
phone only upset her: we sounded so far away. "Letters," she
wrote, "are clear and measured forms of thought. I only wish
you'd have the patience to write a few. In a letter one weeds out
the necessary from the *not*." A lot of my mail was from her, and
I found myself going to the post office as little as once a month.

I preferred to use the phone; I felt more protected by the
fleeting aspect of speech. I called Mother and Father from time
to time; I called Clarissa and Michael once a week. Clarissa said
to me, "We used to talk more and I miss you." I said, "I'm sorry."
She was quiet.

As for Penn, I'd have called him if it had been possible. His
letters were all posted from different places: Red Hook, Little
Dix, Montego Bay. He wrote that he missed me. And I missed
him. Every day after work, I set a place for him at the kitchen
table. I even cleared a drawer for him in the bedroom. Then, in
October, he appeared.

I was in the kitchen, sorting through mail. He rapped on the window and let himself in the back door. He looked skinny and darker than me. He held three canvas bags; they smelled of the sea. Out of one he took four starfish, two sea urchins and a pink conch. He placed them in front of me, spaced them several inches apart; he told me I could have all but one. But I chose only one, the smallest starfish.

He said, "You finally look a little older, maybe 'cause you're thinner, but it agrees with you. Tell me everything you've been doing, everything."

"I've applied to botany schools. And I've also been translating poetry and training horses."

"And I've become an astronaut."

"Why didn't you call before you came?" I said.

"You're not happy I'm here?"

"Why are you here?"

"I know I've been away for a long while," he said. I noticed a scar, shaped like a tuning fork, on his lower thigh. "But I loved being on a boat. There's no distractions; you just keep the sail. And at every port, I found something cool to do. Once, I even helped build a boat. But now, after all that time at sea . . . I don't know. Things feel different. I met some women, you know, one, two—"

"Please, don't tell me."

"Honestly, there was only one who . . . Maybe two . . . You're perspiring all over."

I asked Mitchell to give Penn a job. Mitchell had begun a helicopter service to take the hotel guests to and from the surrounding islands. The helicopter landed on the well-paved roof of the hotel; the pilot was the pharmacist Tack. For forty dollars a day, Penn brought on drinks and cleaned the vehicle after every trip.

"I want to learn how to fly it," he said. It was a cloudy morning. We were sitting in the stone hut Mitchell had built for the guests. When there were no passengers, Mitchell used the helicopter to carry supplies. That day, several rosebushes for his garden were arriving. "Tack tells me I can get my license on Saint Thomas," Penn said. "Would you fly with me?"

"I prefer planes," I said.

"You know, Cora, you can go to very private places with a copter. They're kind of sly."

Mitchell appeared, just as Tack lowered the helicopter to the ground. After Tack and Penn unloaded all the rosebushes—the smell made me feel giddy—Penn brought out several boxes of long-stem roses. "For your love, Mister Willet?" he said as he handed the boxes to Mitchell.

"I didn't order those," Mitchell said. "But no matter. Give Tack a box, and give me a box, and keep the rest for you and Cora."

There were over twelve boxes left. "Why don't we return them?" I said. "It's their mistake."

"Waste of time," Mitchell told me and then hurried away.

Tack took out a jackknife and used it to scrape mud off his shoe. He said, "I don't need any more roses. They grow right outside my door. You lovebirds keep them." He walked back to the helicopter.

"What's Willet expect in return for all he gives?" Penn said as he broke an already crushed rose in half. He tossed away the bud and put the stem in his mouth. When I didn't answer him, he ran off to fetch the vacuum cleaner.

Then I said, "He expects what he gets: nothing."

After several weeks together, Penn and I fell into the habit of staying up late, chatting. One night, he said, "You've started to talk in your sleep. But I can't understand what you're saying. It sounds like a prayer." A candle was burning on the dresser. The wax smelled strong, like charcoal, as it dropped onto the wood.

"I don't believe in God, so I'm not praying." I figured I was too timid to tell Penn during the day whatever it was that I unknowingly mumbled during the night.

"I never believed in God either," he said, "even before my father died. I thought of my father a lot when I was on the boat.

But I couldn't remember certain things. And without my memories, I couldn't get to how I really felt about him. One night, I was so sad or angry or whatever, I tried to scream at the top of my lungs, but this wail came out instead; it was long and it scared me. . . . Y'know, it was a terrible sound and I was feeling pathetic."

The candle went out; I got up to relight it. I said, "If you'd made no sound, you would have been pathetic."

"Will you blow out the candle? It smells and I don't want to smell anything but you."

In the morning, I woke up to someone pounding on our bedroom door; I thought it had to be Mitchell. I slipped on my underwear, and as I started reaching for my robe, Terrence swung open the door. He turned away, apologized, but I saw that he was nervous and perspiring. He left the bedroom and said loudly, "Mitchell Willet's dead."

I got back into bed and covered myself.

"What happened?" Penn said to Terrence.

"A heart attack, a stroke. I really don't know. I went over there this morning and found him lying on the couch. He was only sixty-six."

Mitchell had told me he was fifty-three.

The next day, I wanted to pack up Mitchell's house, as if my being there would make me feel close to him again. I asked Terrence and Penn to help me. Mitchell had no relatives.

Terrence was wrapping Mitchell's wineglasses in newspaper when he said, "You guys take the bird. Did you know a willet is a kind of shorebird? The perfect name for someone who was always acting as if he had a little nest to protect."

I said, "What little nest?"

"Bat Island, naturally," Terrence said. "I remember he once told this family—they were wealthy Cubans exiled years ago by Castro—that the house they wanted to buy had just been outbid by another couple. It wasn't true. But Willet was one of those successful men who always felt threatened by other successful men."

I excused myself to go outside, where I tore off the burned fringes of the wick on a torch. It was that point in the afternoon when the birds seem too exhausted from their morning song to make any sound. I heard Penn say, "Always something about him I didn't trust."

Why was I the only one who had trusted Mitchell? I knew he wasn't entirely admirable. Yet I respected him and his reclusiveness; I tended to be reclusive, too. I glanced at Penn's shadow behind the window. I thought: He knows me well; he can damage me. Mitchell hadn't known me half as well and had never tried to find out more about me. He seemed not to care if I—or anyone—discovered something shameful about him. I could hear him say: *Dislike* me; I'll trust you more. Was that what I admired most about him?

I went back into the house. Terrence told me where the bird's food was. Then he left, taking a bag of golf balls he'd found in the closet.

Penn and I packed up Mitchell's clothes in the bedroom; next, we cleaned the cabinets in the study. I was touching all of Mitchell's possessions. Some looked as if they had belonged to his wife—a collection of Wedgwood teacups. There were cassette tapes of Berlioz, Beethoven, Gershwin, Coltrane, Ellington; an old pipe made of some kind of antler. I piled everything into boxes. I was quiet.

Penn sat next to me. "You seem so torn up and . . . I know Mitchell Willet gave you a lot. I'm not sure whether . . . I mean, there was nothing more going on between the two of you, I should . . ."

I pushed him away. "I've thought of no one but you," I said, "even when I've been in bed with someone else."

"Then you'll marry me someday?"

"Women in my family collapse under contracts." My heart beat faster. I thought of Amelia Eliot and Father and Mother.

Penn came close to me and grabbed my hand. "You're silly. What about having children?"

"Children . . . well, children are a big thought. They're so loyal when they're young, and then—"

"Just answer me."

"There isn't one answer."

"Then give me a few."

I didn't like his cornering me. Not at all. "You're hurting my hand," I said. When he loosened his grip, I said, "Think of my mother and how she sees 'children.' You heard what Michael said on the phone; she's put all our photographs in the upstairs hall, she's tagged our possessions with dates and notes: 'Clarissa's record collection, 1965 to 1972.' She's still trying to preserve the family."

"I'm not talking about your mother. She doesn't rule you anymore—"

"So now maybe you rule me?"

He started taping the boxes and looked away from me.

I said, "My sickness will come back. And I don't want you to see it. I'll dislike who I am again. Which was all right when I was younger. But by now I should know getting sick isn't my fault." I felt strangely calm.

He said, "But you do know."

The first day of December brought a sensational wind and, I believed, a new species of bats to the east side of the island, which was beginning to turn green again. These bats ate all of Mitchell's overripe tomatoes and so prevented his garden from completely spoiling.

Penn had just got his pilot license. He wanted to fly the helicopter one Sunday afternoon. We were getting our chores out of the way, mowing the yard, watering the trees. I was drenching the tops of the palm trees; as the wind sprayed water back onto my face, I considered what it would be like to have Penn around permanently. I'd be a teacher of some kind; maybe I'd come home at noon after teaching math to first-grade boys and girls. Penn would already be home, showering off salt. He'd have a few airplanes, two helicopters. . . . I threatened to get him wet; he seemed preoccupied.

He caught the hose and twisted the top into a knot.

"There's something wrong," I said.

He dropped the hose at my feet. "I was thinking about your views on marriage and I thought there's something I should probably tell you. When I was in Saint Bart's, I met this woman; she was twenty-five. One night we got really drunk. And TNT put on his captain's hat and pretended he could marry us."

"Penn, what if it's legal?"

"She reminded me of you. For me, she was you. I knew it meant nothing. It's legal only if the couple believes the captain has the authority to marry them. We knew our captain didn't."

I was watering my bare feet. My heels pressed into the soil. "So you've confessed and you feel less guilty. Now explain to me all this confessing of past sins. Let's say I did something I regret; why shouldn't I keep my mistakes as my own? If I share them, you'll absolve me of the guilt?"

"Yes."

Thinking he sounded too victorious, I slumped against a tree. How had this stunning woman of twenty-five held his arm while playacting bride-to-be?

"Come on," he said, "let's go for a ride." He took out his new license.

"I don't think so." I walked into the house without looking back.

Lying on the floor, I imagined a tireless woman hunting all over the islands for Penn. Pluto was on top of the television. I got up to scratch his crown; he bent his neck, and his feathers ruffled; I petted him for some time, as if the bird's tranquillity could be touched and taken. Then I heard the helicopter. I ran out to the terrace. The helicopter was directly above me. Penn started dropping roses, dozens of them. Had he been secretly storing them? Roses fell, and hibiscus and daffodils were mixed in with them, and they all fluttered down, over the house and over the yard. The wind snipped the leaves off the branches; loose petals flew around me. I stood facing the sky, the flowers still falling.

*   *   *

I break up a lump of sugar that Penn spilled yesterday morning and left, typically, on the breakfast table. It's about 8:00 A.M.; Penn's in bed, with sunstroke. The temperature has been in the nineties, unusually high for the first week of December; nonetheless, I'm delighted to be missing winter. I clean up the sugar and then the rest of the kitchen. The kitchen door is open. Through it, I still see a few shriveled petals fluttering on the ground. I remember the day Penn first appeared through the door, a dirty beach bag swinging from his shoulder . . . the day Mother burst into the kitchen to tell Father that Mitchell was falling in love with her . . . the day I first got sick, though I'd never been seriously ill in this house. . . . Suddenly I want to rush to Penn, to lie beside him, just to hear him breathe. But I tell myself to stay where I am; and I do.

Keys to Keep

Anna-Marie and Paul Benton lived on the ground floor of a brownstone on West Eighty-ninth Street. When I first went there, Anna-Marie told me, "Paul's in Guatemala again, photographing orphans who live in a garbage dump."

While he was gone, I saw her almost every night, and now we were in her bed, warm. I told her that the bed was beautiful; she told me that it was French Baroque and that Paul had surprised her: he'd had it sent to her one morning when he was in East Africa. "Wasn't he thoughtful?" she said. "So I could sleep in a new bed alone for a month?"

I looked out the window to where in the warm months she grew roses and chrysanthemums. The ground was buckled in places; the wind swept up bits of dirt and came through the open window, blowing on the irises I'd brought, which stood in a vase on the sill.

"Let's shut the window," I said. "It's going to snow."

She reached over my chest, took my keys from the night table and sat up. She threw my keys out the window.

I said, "I need those."

"Not this week you don't. I'll give you my extra set."

"And then Paul returns?" I looked up at the cluster of roses carved in the center of the headboard.

She turned on her stomach and didn't answer.

Later that night, we were lying on the rug and she was telling me, ". . . and every Christmas I wrapped gifts for Missus Meropollis."

"Meropollis?" I sipped some champagne we had left over from the night before.

"The Meropollises lived in a very big house at the end of a private drive. Their daughter Rachel was one of my best friends, and she had seven brothers and sisters and they all got so many Christmas gifts from the parents. The Meropollises paid me to wrap them." Her hands went up to her face. "I was one jealous girl." Her fingers slipped down her neck, her fingernails skating along. "What do you care about the suburbs of Chicago?"

"I've never been to Chicago."

"One day you'll have to go just to see the Meropollis castle." She laughed and I saw how comfortable she was with me, but then she whispered, "Don't look so troubled. I'll cook you dinner tomorrow."

I said, "You trouble me."

"Of course I do."

I went to get an extra set of keys from my super, Mr. Warlow, and he said to me, "I never see you. You have a nice girl?"

I went upstairs.

I didn't know what to do with myself, what to do without Anna-Marie, so I called you, for some reason. You sounded as if you were between sleeping and waking, your voice half disguised by static. I said I'd become lazy, filling my time with meaningless activities, and you told me, "Use the activities for your acting."

I said, "It'd be good to see you." And I wasn't sure whether I meant that or not.

The next day, I was going to buy more irises for Anna-Marie, but I bought a small silver-edged hand mirror instead. I had some money from having chauffeured people to and from Greenwich. I hadn't minded the job, hadn't minded being fired, either, when I accidentally scraped the car against another on the highway. Now I was painting the insides of houses with a man who liked to tell me how the right formula ($F = ma$) helped determine the condition of the paint in ten years. I didn't really listen as he spoke about time and forces altering surfaces and he didn't seem to mind whether or not I listened. I was always thinking about Anna-Marie and wanted to talk about her while I worked, but how to explain her to someone I simply painted houses with? There was much about her I couldn't explain to myself: why stay with Paul, a man who was drawn to places Anna-Marie was scared of? Did he have affairs? And had she before me?

At school, when I did pay attention, it was mostly to the other students. I'd been watching one particular woman for some time. She wasn't talented and I saw that when she wanted to hide her lack of confidence she'd be too gentle about finding fault with another student's acting. That pretense sickened me and I disregarded all her virtues. In my spare time, I began looking to catch someone in a deceitful act, no matter how small the betrayal; in the morning, waiting for the light to change, I'd noticed a girl admiring another boy while she held her boyfriend's hand.

I didn't go to auditions. I told myself, carrying Anna-Marie's gift under my arm and passing a sanitation truck that had left some trash on the ground (how was Paul feeling as he took shots of children in a dump?), I wasn't ready for auditions yet, I just wasn't ready.

*   *   *

Anna-Marie opened the door and said, "I just got here." She had on a red blouse and a gray skirt and high black boots. "I had a late lunch with a friend of Paul's so I didn't have time to shop. You're disappointed, I know. . . ."

"Here," I said and handed her the gift. "What do you want to do? We can't go out. God forbid someone should see you with me. What do we do?"

She smiled, opened the box and took out the mirror. "This is lovely. I'll carry this with me so I can glance at my imperfections anywhere." She looked in the mirror. "Seriously, it's lovely. . . ."

"I feel horrible; I don't know what's the matter with me," I said.

"You remind me of this Irish man I once dated, Charles O'Connor."

"Last week you told me I reminded you of John Somebody."

"Yes, maybe John Reynolds." She apologized once more about dinner and turned on some piano music from the stereo inside the den. I thought about the time I'd asked about the den, the door always closed, and she'd said that the den was Paul's office.

The first time I'd been with her, even the second, I didn't care what happened between us, or if I ever saw her again, but now I found myself saying, "I want to take you home to meet my sisters, believe it or not."

She blushed, and she wasn't easily embarrassed. "Wouldn't that be nice."

"Maybe we can go away together," I said. "To Paris, to Rio, somewhere bright and loud, where there are a lot of people."

"Go away? Maybe this is getting to be too much; maybe we should just stop."

"You say that so easily. Have you said that before?"

"What are you talking about?"

"Have you cheated on Paul before?"

She took the Scotch bottle out of the bar and poured herself a glass. "No, and even if I have, it's my business."

"But I'd like the truth and you know the reason."

"Michael, what does reason have to do with us?"

I made her dinner, and after we ate, she said, "Tomorrow I have to go to Nice. Paul has a show at a gallery there and he'll be giving a lecture. He's flying in from Guatemala. He gets so anxious about speeches. Did I ever tell you about the time I wanted to fly to Nice and ended up in Marseilles? There'd been a fire at the airport in Nice, so they put us up in a hotel near the Marseilles airport. I met this woman and she knew everyone I knew: we chatted about the Meropollises, the Howes, everyone."

She was going away tomorrow? I said, "You're hung up on this Meropollis woman."

She said, "The other day I found out Missus Meropollis is dying. . . . But what's with me? You get me thinking about the damnedest things. You say you want to do what most couples do. I have news for you: they talk, and it's an exchange. Tell me something about you, something you used to do."

I said, "When did you find out you were going away?"

She started clearing the table and almost dropped a plate. "I should have told you the other night."

Anna-Marie was supposed to be in Nice for a week, but soon three weeks passed without a call from her. I went for walks. One day, I walked to Anna-Marie's block and there was a wreath on the door of her brownstone. The building had no grand moldings, as the two on either side of it had, but the gate was black and elaborate. Two keys were needed to get through. I used the extra set of keys she'd forgotten to get back from me and I thought: What if Paul's home? what if they're both home, with the lights out?

I let myself in and turned off the alarm, which was hidden behind a fake fuse box. Someone had cleaned the windows in the living room. I remembered when Anna-Marie had thrown my keys out the bedroom window. The keys were still lying outside, under snow. A blue cardigan was thrown over the back of the couch; in an ashtray, a yellow cigarette butt had been dissected, and I picked at the shreds. Yes, someone had been there recently.

I opened the door to the den, expecting to see Paul and Anna-Marie making love. I switched on the light. The desk was covered with photography books containing shots of partially clothed women, old men and dilapidated shacks near a ravine. There was a picture of Paul and Anna-Marie on the desk. He was blond, blue-eyed. Dull.

I went into the bedroom; the bed was neatly made. I was about to leave, but a sweet chemical smell hung in the room, and I knew it belonged to Paul. Then I wanted to stay and I went into the kitchen, opened all the cabinets and found a toolbox; it had Paul's name on it. Back in the bedroom, I started unscrewing the headboard from the metal frame that held the mattress, and then I unscrewed the footboard from the frame. I leaned the two pieces against the wall, and moving quietly, I went back to the bed and started to take apart the metal frame but then stopped myself, leaving the mattress half-leaning on the floor. I opened all the windows as wide as they could go, thinking I had to get the sweet smell out of the room. A breeze came in. I leaned on the mattress, focusing on a distant point in the garden, waiting for . . . Paul or Anna-Marie?

At home, I unplugged the phone and picked up a play by a fellow student. It was an experimental play.

I wondered if Anna-Marie would have me arrested. If Penn were here, he'd laugh. He'd say, Just, you've done it again.

Why hadn't she called me?

I was hungry and went into the kitchen, but there was nothing to eat. There were a few acting books on the kitchen counter. I thought of a short story by Chekhov, "The Lady with a Pet Dog." In it, a married man seduces a married woman; the man has already had many affairs. The woman feels guilty over her love for him yet still is in love with him, and in time, he falls in love with her.

I left the kitchen and started going through my desk drawer, looking for some pot, but instead I found a photograph of us all. There you were, there was Mother. . . . I was standing between Cora and Mother. I ripped out the image of myself and threw it in the trash.

She still hadn't called and another week passed; her silence seemed senseless to me. To clear my mind, I played ice hockey on a frozen lake in Westport with friends, but I fell and twisted my ankle. That night in bed, my ankle throbbing, I poured myself some Scotch and called Anna-Marie again. The phone machine answered and I hung up, almost breaking the receiver.

She called a few hours later from a phone on the street, and she sounded curt. Something was tapping the receiver and I pictured her long fingernails, as she said, "May I come over? I'm on the corner."

She walked in and threw her purse on the unmade bed. "Look at this place," she said. She took off her fur hat. I saw she'd cut her hair short. "I may not respect Paul sometimes, which is my problem; that has nothing to do with you. But I care for him and I don't want him hurt. Thank god, I came home first. So nothing was proved. You've only made me feel very sorry for you. That's something I've never felt for Paul."

"Ah, so I made you feel something new."

She looked around at the blanket on the floor, the shoes near the bathroom, the books piled in the corner. She sat by me on the bed, picked up one of my shirts from the floor and put the shirt beside her.

"Forgive me," I said.

"I just couldn't see you. And I'm unhappy about that. Maybe I've always been unhappy. Yet we are definitely that way together, aren't we? Why did you sneak into my home?"

I didn't answer; I liked the quiet.

"Michael?"

For the moment, I didn't know how to talk to her; I just wanted her to leave. I took her keys out of my pocket and pressed them into her hand.

"You're scaring me," she said. "I'm trying to understand you. I know how you feel, and you should know: I feel it, too—"

"Stop," I said and then abruptly stood.

After Anna-Marie left, I called you. You weren't in and I let the phone ring for a while. I hung up and called Mother. She said, Where have you been? I feel as if I don't have a son. . . .

And I said I'd see her soon.

I called Clarissa. She was out.

I called Cora and Penn; Cora answered. She said, "What's wrong with you?"

"Where's Penn?"

"He's working, but what's wrong?" She waited for me to answer.

After a pause, I said, "People talk and talk and I can't tell what they mean anymore."

I said goodbye to Cora and then went right into the bathroom. The phone rang, the machine picked up and I heard Anna-Marie's voice: "I've thought of—"

I shut the bathroom door. Behind an aspirin bottle I found a razor blade, one I'd used to scrape paint off surfaces when I'd first started working. I turned my head and slid the blade over my palm and wrist. Lightly. I cut the palm, not deep, and felt not even a little pain. Then, feeling sick, I dropped the blade onto the floor.

Mr. Warlow was staring down at me, his stale breath waking me. "Christ," he said, "I haven't seen you for days. I hadda fix your pipes. There's a bad leak in the apartment below you. Lucky I had another set of keys and let myself in. Now, boy, do you want me to call a doctor? You look like hell."

My palm felt stuck to the bottom sheet, but at least my hand was hidden under the blanket. And the day was . . . ? "I have the flu," I said. "I just have to rest. Fix your pipes and let me rest."

"They're fixed. But I have to come back tomorrow. Listen,

you want me to paint the place? The rent's going up next year, don't forget."

"I won't be renewing my lease. I'll be leaving," I said, surprised at what sounded like a reasonable decision.

"Fine, fine. I got plenty of people who want to live here. But clean this place up. Jesus, I found aspirin, papers and whatever in heaven's name you got on your bathroom floor. Looks like blood to me. What'd you—fall?"

I walk by her house, on the opposite side of the street. It's about noon, and ice covers the ground, trapping papers and cigarette butts. Christmas and Hanukkah decorations already hang from streetlamps and in store windows. I walk toward Central Park, looking only in front of me while rubbing my clean-shaven chin.

But soon I'm walking back, by her house again, still on the opposite side of the street. . . .

In no time I'm at the Sheep Meadow, pacing along the fence, watching two dogs run loose beyond the meadow; some teenagers are leaning on the fence and they look at me. My stride must appear smooth to them as I slow down to watch one black Labrador chase the other. But what's this I feel? Elation? . . . No— something closer to the circumspection of that dog as it crouches down to pounce. Gets the other to run.

A Clear Map

Lee is district manager of five stores in Puerto Rico. He wants to be director of store operations. He has moved up quickly. As for me, I'm pleased not to have a job.

We have a three-bedroom apartment in Old San Juan, with a view of the ocean. A poor fishing village, La Perla, tilts on a slope by the shore. I keep track of the buildings that go up to my right, along Isla Verde. They're pink and lime condominiums, with playgrounds and pools.

We still have our cat, Ruby. She has slipped out once or twice for the night. She comes back in early morning, when a partial mist covers the water. I like the mist. It's almost always there.

It was mid-December 1980. Lee suggested we drive through the Cordillera Central before the New Year. He wanted to go to

Ponce. I wanted to take a short trip and buy a *coco frío* at a road stand. I mapped out our route.

We left at six Saturday morning. Our daughter, Bridget, was in the car seat, asleep. She was four and a half weeks old. Lee had wanted to leave her with Dad. I liked her to be with me. Bridget has blond hair, Lee's full lips and a beauty mark on her left cheek. Labor had been easy, two hours at the most. But it came early. She spent two weeks in an incubator. Lee stayed by my bed and pulled out strands of his hair without realizing it. I blew the hairs from his fingers. "This happens to babies all the time," I told him.

Our first stop was Cayey. We bought some orange juice at a canteen. Most of the stores were closed, so we drove on to Ponce. When we got there, we parked in the shade. The town was clean and cooled by clouds.

Lee rested his head on the wheel. He watched me as I nursed Bridget. She was tugging at my left nipple. He took out a map. "Around Lent, Ponce has a festival. We'll have to go," he said. "Men dress up in devil costumes and wear masks and then chase children. The kids taunt them with rhymes, but the devils have *vejigas*. That's the bladder of a pig or a calf. They tap the kids with the *vejigas* if they're not quick with their rhymes."

"I should think that would terrify a child."

"No, no, no. . . . It'll do us all good to go to the carnival. We should know every charm of the island."

"I'm hungry," I said. We found a coffee shop and had break-fast. I thought of how much Mom had liked Ponce. But the town had changed in the past few years. There were more stores and fast-food places. She wouldn't like it now, I thought. Of course, I still call her my mother. Most of the time, I'm not bitter. I'm comforted by knowing: Amelia's mother died in the sixties; Amelia's father also died; he used to shoot quail; Amelia has an aunt somewhere in Maine. And Amelia is buried in Boston. I haven't gone to her grave yet. When I think of her as once having been alive, I can't always imagine how she'd move or look. But I can hear how she'd speak. She'd have a determined voice. She'd never whisper.

After breakfast, Lee and I walked to the Ponce museum. The museum was hot. I went to my favorite painting, F. Leighton's *Flaming June*. It shows a young woman sleeping and the ocean calm behind her. We left when Lee complained of the heat.

We took Highway 10 to the mountains. Tiny purple and pink flowers grew along the road.

Lee said, "I wonder how high this mountain is." A truck came from the other direction. It was going fast and honked at us. The road had sharp curves, so we drove slowly.

"Remember how you used to make up facts?" I asked.

"I never made them up. How's Bridget? I still wish we'd left her home."

"She's not causing problems." I glanced back at Bridget. She was staring out the window.

We came to a small town. It had only a bakery and a coffee shop and a small junkyard with a sign, JUNKER, dangling from a chain. Behind the bakery, there were three or four beat-up Chryslers and Oldsmobiles. A teenage boy was sitting on the hood of a Mustang, smoking a cigarette. His headlights had the face of Jesus painted on them.

"Something's going on here," Lee said and stopped the car.

Behind the cars there was a group of men. Lee walked up to the crowd, waving for me to follow. I had Bridget in my arms. The men were about to watch a cockfight. I stayed where I was, while Lee fit himself between a man wearing a straw hat and a man with hair that stood up. Lee had on yellow Bermuda shorts. I heard the squawks and shouts. Bridget began to cry. I got into the car, rolled up the windows and started the car. I'd never seen a cockfight. Dad hadn't cared for them. Mom used to cringe when she heard the men cheer.

Lee came back. He looked disgusted. "That was quick," he said and then shut the door.

"I can't believe you watched that."

"A guy at the office was telling me it's an ancient sport, a gentlemen's sport. All the bets are verbal. You can trace it to classical Greece."

He backed the car up. A man was carrying the dead cock into a house. Its crest looked like wet ribbons.

"Maybe they eat them," Lee said. "Maybe they don't go to waste."

Lee drove with his left knee leaning on the armrest of the door. A half hour up the mountain, we saw a sign: SANTERO/SANTOS— ANTONIO JESUS MARTÍNEZ.

"A real saint-maker. Let's stop." Lee pulled over.

"Why not say a prayer, too?" I said.

He looked at Bridget and said, "We'll buy her a saint."

All the doors and windows of the *santero*'s house were open. The room was painted pink. A wooden cross hung on the wall. In the corner, a man sat at a table. He was heavy and had a bottle of Corona beer before him. He was carving a block of wood. A fan made his shirttails flutter. He nodded to us and pointed to a shelf by the door. On the shelf stood a row of finished saints. Two were women with a lion at their feet. They had a card in front of them that said "Santa María." Next to them were four saints. Their card said "San Juan el Bautista." Those saints were clothed in a skin. Below them, on a larger shelf, were ten other saints, with the card "San Francisco." They carried a bird.

Lee pulled himself up a stool. He talked about our drive and the cockfight. The *santero* nodded during Lee's pauses. Lee told him we'd just moved to the island. Then he took a San Francisco off the shelf.

I said to Lee, "He seems to be partial to Saint Francis." And I whispered, "What do you call a saint when he's not taking care of the poor and sick?"

"Fired," Lee said. He told the *santero*, "We're not the religious kind."

The *santero* waved his hand. He got up and opened a box. In it were several straw hats. The *santero* said, "For magic." He put the hat on and an Independentista flag popped out of the top. He said, "Twenty dollars for you."

Lee said, "No thanks." He'd voted for the statehood party in the November elections.

The *santero* opened a second box. He took out another hat and put it on Lee's head. A United States flag popped out of the hat. "For the American. Twenty-five dollars."

Lee said, "My wife doesn't like me in hats."

The *santero* began speaking in Spanish. He said his shop might as well be shut down. On occasion, a shop owner from Ponce or San Juan bought a few saints from him.

"Maybe we'll buy one," Lee said to the *santero*. "My wife," he went on in careful Spanish. "She doesn't think we should have one if we don't believe." He slipped into English but kept speaking to the *santero*. "Me, I'm Jewish. What I learn, I learn from my father. He's suddenly become kosher. It's a new thing with him. He grows stricter as he grows older. And I respect him for it. Which is saying a lot. I've never really had much respect for him. But now he knows his history and where he comes from. I'm, without a doubt, a lousy Jew. You must see it all the time: people who don't believe stick together. And here you are—your sales way down because of people like us."

The *santero* laughed. I didn't think he'd understood Lee. I was feeling hot. I said to Lee, "You love to talk for me."

He said, "If you'd only be friendlier . . ."

The *santero* picked up another hat and set it on my head. The Independentista flag popped up. "For you," he said, "fifteen dollars."

I gave the hat back. "I'll wait outside," I said to Lee.

"But, Clarissa, here's your chance to learn. There are probably more saints than you've ever imagined. I bet there's a Saint Bridget. Isn't there, Señor Martínez?" Lee said and picked up a carving tool out of a tin pot.

The *santero* said, *"Hay un santo para todos."* He went back to his sculpting. He left the hats on top of a box.

Lee said, "A saint for everyone, Clarissa! Why shouldn't there be?"

The *santero* lightly slashed the five wounds into the wooden figure he'd just carved. He said, *"El Cristo."* His tone had become biting, I thought.

I left the shop. Outside, the breeze felt good. I heard Lee say, "Do you have a Santa Clarissa? My wife's birthday is coming up."

Lee walked out of the house with a small brown package under his arm. He'd chosen a Santa María. He said, "That man in there has some ungodly merchandise. Where else shall we go?" He put the wrapped saint next to Bridget.

"Let's just go."

Lee tapped the wheel to the rhythm of the salsa on the radio. It started to rain. Soon the rain was falling hard. He said, "We'll stop until this lets up."

As we headed around a corner, we hit a fallen branch. The car swerved into the mountain wall. Lee's knee struck the door. Bridget howled in the back.

"Is she okay?" Lee was holding his shoulder.

"She's all right," I said and climbed over the seat into the back to look her over. The car rocked.

He said, "Let me have her, please. God, I couldn't see."

The car then creaked into a ditch. The windshield was cracked on my side. As we shifted to get more comfortable, the car rocked again. The tire seemed stuck in the ditch. Bridget was crying.

We made two decisions. Lee would walk back to the *santero*'s and call for help. And Lee and I wouldn't blame one another. The inside of the car was cool. I fed Bridget while Lee went to the phone.

"I'm sorry," he said when he came back. He unstuck his shirt from his stomach. "The umbrella didn't help much." He took off his shirt. I handed him a spare T-shirt I'd packed for Bridget. He dried his chest with it. He was shivering.

I opened the glove compartment to look for the car registration. I took out a neat stack of papers, the registration lying on top.

"What's this?" Lee said and slipped a Polaroid out of the stack. It showed Lee carving a piece of meat inside an Isla freezer. "Doesn't even look like me, does it? I don't like Polaroids; they're ugly. The image is never as sharp as you'd like it to be."

"They serve their purpose." I thought the photograph looked a lot like him.

He placed the Polaroid on the seat and said, "I heard a funny story at the office."

"Good, tell me. We could use a laugh, but first put down something so I can change her."

He got Bridget's changing blanket and placed it on the seat between us. He said, "Bob told me he went to the Caribe Casino with this girl he'd just met. She tells him she's never played craps before. He says to her: I'll give you three hundred dollars; you do as I say and keep what you win. The thing is, she's a virgin at the game, and virgins bring him luck."

"I'm sure he didn't put it that nicely."

"So he goes into the casino and they start to play. With every roll he's yelling: 'I got a virgin here!' Turns out he wins twenty dollars and the virgin wins five thousand."

I said that seemed fair.

"I feel so protected living here," he told me, glancing at the Polaroid. "I mean, first, we live at your father's house, we move in his circles—last night's dinner, a perfect example— and now we're spoiled. We can't even go for a ride without getting ourselves in trouble."

"I suppose you'll never forgive my father for keeping the truth from me." I hadn't expected him to act as if nothing had happened. I'd expected him to talk to me about Amelia more than he had.

"It has nothing to do with what I can forgive," he said quickly. "I just wouldn't have made his choice, but then again, I wouldn't have slept with a woman who was engaged. . . . Have you ever cheated on me?"

"Do you really want to know?"

"You make it sound as if you have."

I taped up Bridget's diaper. "Have you?"

"I never wanted anyone else that much," he said. "You need to have a tremendous desire to go through with it. I didn't think you had such a desire."

"I haven't cheated on you."

Bridget was smiling, clutching the sleeve of Lee's wet shirt. I wondered if Lee had a Polaroid of her, too. I started looking for one in the stack of papers. I found a note I'd written to Lee and read it aloud, " 'We need tea, strawberry preserves (maybe try guava?). Better get both. Rissa.' " I said, "Did you mean to save this?"

"Why don't you ever write 'love'?" he asked.

"Lee, this is just a note."

"But you never write it." He took Bridget from me. I didn't know what to say, but he said, "I'd leave you if I found out you had an affair. And if I had one, I'd want you to leave me."

"I don't know if you'd leave."

"Actually, I don't know where I'd go. Here I am: away from my family, working for your father, and I don't know why I'm doing any of it anymore."

I said, "I thought you loved it."

"Yes, but I'm not doing it for me."

By the time we get home, it's dark. Lee is limping a little. He says, "I think I hurt my knee."

"Let me look at it."

But he tells me he wants to change his clothes and then bathe Bridget. He takes her into her room.

I unwrap the *santo* and put it on the coffee table. But I don't like it there. I then place it on a high bookshelf, next to a pair of wooden candlesticks. I think of Bridget crying in the car. It was the first time there was terror in her cry. I'm more than sorry for that.

I sort through the weekend mail to steady my hands. There's a bill from the electric company, a bill from the pediatrician. And there's a letter from Mom, the second she has sent in a week. This one she has sent by express mail.

December 19, 1980

Dearest Clarissa and Lee,

The other day I got word that I was to inherit Bat Island. Imagine that! We all knew Mitchell Willet had no children, no relatives, and apparently, he was greatly taken by me. What a sweet devil! He has truly changed the course of my tiresome life. I think of him, sometimes, as a passing fancy I regret having dismissed. I hate to think he felt sorry for me, but if so . . .

My loves, an island! I just told Michael the news. He said he'd think I'd want nothing to do with the place because of its memories. But I said I've only held on to the fond memories.

I'll use Mitch's house whenever I visit, which means I *won't* meddle with your father, but I can't help smiling. . . .

I've written Cora, too, though I've yet to hear from her. She seems to stay quite healthy there, keeping the grounds neat. Won't little Bridget be surprised to see her first bat?

God bless. Miss you all.

Love and kisses,

Mom.

P.S. I think everyone should have an island of one's own— don't you agree?

About the Author

LORI TOPPEL grew up in Puerto Rico and now lives in New York City. *Three Children* is her first published novel.